Murphy's Herd

Also by the Author

Murphy's Gold
Murphy

Murphy's Herd

Gary Paulsen

Walker and Company
New York

First published in the United States of America in 1989
by Walker Publishing Company, Inc.

Published simultaneously in Canada by Thomas Allen & Son
Canada, Limited, Markham, Ontario

Library of Congress Cataloging-in-Publication Data

Paulsen, Gary.
Murphy's herd / Gary Paulsen.
p. cm.
ISBN 0-8027-4094-4
I. Title.
PS3566.A834M87 1989   88-34871
813'.54—dc19   CIP

Printed in the United States of America

10 9 8 7 6 5 4 3 2 1

Murphy's Herd

CHAPTER 1

SOMETIMES later he would remember this ride north and his life in the valley with Midge and it would seem to be the only gentle thing in his life.

Before coming to the valley Al Murphy had resigned his sheriff job in Cincherville. He and Midge had left with no real plan or place to go, had just let the mules pull the wagon north until they were tired and had worked sweat on their flanks and were getting stubborn enough to kick at the trace chains. Then Murphy pulled them off the twin-rutted northern trail into better grass and called them to a stop—although to be honest, there wasn't much calling. When he quit slapping them across the rumps with the lines, they stopped as if they'd been nailed to the ground.

Murphy climbed down from the wagon. "Not much for mules, are they?" he said up to Midge. "We haven't made fifteen miles all day. If you stand on the wagon seat you can still see Cincherville."

She looked down and smiled at him. "Does it matter as long as we're going?"

"No, I don't guess that it does."

He paused, one hand resting on her leg and the other over on the rump of the near mule. The mule fidgeted under his touch and leaned against him, wanting the harness off. Flies worked around the animals' tails.

Murphy and Midge had been all day under a flat blue sky, and even with Midge wearing an old straw hat—he

1

had teased her about looking like a rail-busted dirt farmer—her face had taken so much sun that the freckles all but exploded on her. The freckles went across her nose and down her cheeks and neck and disappeared into the open throat of her dress.

"You look good," he said simply. "Good enough to marry."

"No," she said, but her eyes were light and liked the compliment. "I look like hell—baked and burned like an old loaf of bread—but I'll hold you to the marrying part."

Murphy laughed and locked the wagon brake, out of habit. They were on level ground but it was best to lock it when you started to unharness. Old knowledge from somewhere—where was that? Maybe the army. Yeah. He remembered a private who'd had some shank-mean mules run on him while he was unhooking them and had gotten tangled in the doubletree when they bolted. They'd dragged him so hard there was almost nothing but tatters and bits of meat when Murphy and another trooper finally got them stopped. Somehow the man had lived for almost two days, moaning and rolling in the infirmary, his face and eyes gone and most of his bones broken, before escaping into death.

Mules.

If he and Midge found a place up north he would have to keep the mules and use them, bad as they were, and he wondered as he unhooked them if he really had enough in his sack to run a ranch. Born in the stink of the New York Tenderloin district, kicked west in the army, and since then working the law in broken-down towns, he was amazed at what he didn't know.

He unharnessed the mules and hobbled them and left them to graze while he got them each a gallon of water—it was a dry camp—from a ten-gallon barrel he had in the back of the wagon. Midge was gathering wood for a fire and he watched her for a moment with pleasure. Brown hair, straight and tied back, hung down from the rear of the straw hat. Her arms were round and muscled and tanned where they showed past the sleeves of her dress as she reached for wood.

It was easier to think about what he knew rather than what he didn't know. He knew dark streets and drunks and puke-stink jails. He knew guns and knives and knuckles; he could give pain and he had taken some pain. There were marks and line scars on his body, his nose was thick from having been broken, and a bullet pucker showed on his shoulder, another in his arm, and a crease scar crossed his ribs where a wild drunk had shot him from the rear. That the drunk had died and that Murphy had left worse scars on those who scarred him didn't matter. Didn't help him to know more, or to know anything about real work. Dirt work. Cattle work. Horse work.

I'm dumb, he thought. Just as dumb and slick as a new calf, except for his expertise with a gun. His gun. He wasn't wearing it. Somehow it didn't go with what he and Midge were going to do, so he'd wrapped the Smith in an oil-soaked rag inside some oilcloth and put it in an old wooden dynamite box on the bottom of the wagon bed. He kept a rifle, a .45-70, under the wagon seat for anything they might need a gun for. And he had a double twelve-gauge Greener, with long barrels for prairie chickens, to use when they got north a bit, but the short gun stayed in the box. He had felt light without the Smith all day and there was a dark spot on the side of his pants where the holster had kept the sun from fading the rough material. The son of a bitch will stay in the box until the material matches, he thought suddenly—surprised at the power of the thought—and then I'll take it out and bury it in a hole and run these goddam mules over the hole and never look back . . .

"Find that loaf of bread I brought," Midge called from a fire she had struck with some grass and a match, feeding wood slowly to it. "I'll make some pan gravy and we'll soak it with bread for now. Maybe tomorrow you could get some chickens or a rabbit . . ."

Murphy shook the previous thoughts out of his head and nodded. "I'll walk out to the side tomorrow for a time and see if we can't make some meat." The sun dropped fast once it fell below the mountains rising to the west of them, and darkness seemed to come as soon as the flames got a good start.

Midge took a cast-iron kettle from the wagon—she'd brought a kitchenful of good utensils from the cafe she used to own in Cincherville—and cut some chunks of ham they had saved, which she mixed in with a double handful of flour. When the ham and flour browned off and was smoking slightly, she added water and kept stirring with a fork until she had a rich brown ham gravy. She let some of the water boil off to thicken it and cut slabs of bread and put them on two pie pans she used for plates. Using the edge of her dress for a hot pad she poured gravy over the bread and they ate it with knives and forks while sitting across the fire from each other on bedrolls. Through all of it, the cooking and eating and smiling and burping, Murphy didn't say a word. When it was done he helped her scrape the plates clean and wash them with some of the water from the barrel, still in silence; then they unrolled the bedrolls and made one bed with them next to the fire.

They were married already, and both knew it, felt it,

lived it. They hadn't taken the vows yet before the preacher as Midge wanted, but they were married in their minds and they wanted and needed each other and met in bed. They touched and made love with a quiet intensity, but it was during the time after, before they went to sleep, that Murphy felt so . . . so good.

Always in Cincherville they had pushed marriage away, and when they met to make love they would separate afterwards and Murphy would go back to his room at the hotel. It was silly, and Midge often chided him for it, but he felt it would compromise her to have him move in. Now the other way was right, was clean and right and good, and he reveled in the feeling of having her lie on her back with her head on his arm, looking at the stars and making small talk about the sky, about life, about what they would do when they got north and found the green grass and a place where they could live together.

"We'll have a boy first," she said after a moment of silence filled only with the snap of a pine knot on the fire and the crunch of the mules chewing on the prairie grass. The mules had moved closer with the hard dark, as if wanting company. "You'll need a boy to help with things. Then a girl . . ."

"To help you," Murphy said, cutting in and tickling her ear.

"No. Just because there has to be a girl. She can do anything she wants."

Yes, Murphy thought, if she's like you she can do anything she wants. He was going to tell Midge how much he felt for her then, but he heard her breathing suddenly become even and knew that she was asleep. Just that fast. He pulled the coarse wool point blanket gently up to her chin and touched a calloused finger to her face, her cheek, her nose, her chin, her forehead. Touched her to remember the touch, so that even his skin would remember her skin.

He was tired, bone-tired, from whacking the wagon seat with his behind all day, but he did not want the time to end, did not want the day to end. Then he thought, stupidly without fear and without remembering the rough edges of his life, that he was blessed with good luck: there will be many more days of this, there will be all of the rest of our lives like this. And he let sleep take him.

CHAPTER 2

WITH first light Murphy's eyes snapped open. He was not used to sleeping outside, not used to sleeping in peace, not used to sleeping (just sleeping) with a woman. Blue sky streaked with red and some morning cold sneaking in around the edge of the blanket seemed to be part of the prairie bird songs that came across the grass. Midge slept hard against his shoulder, and when he moved she murmured but remained asleep.

He raised his head and looked around, past the wagon. The mules were gone.

"Damn," he whispered to himself and slid sideways out of the blanket. He'd left his boots upright and they had caught dew and were damp so that he rocked back and forth trying to get them on. The movement awakened Midge. "The mules are gone," he said, standing and stomping down into his boots, tucking his shirt in.

"They couldn't have gone far," she said, rubbing her eyes and straightening her hair. "They were hobbled."

"Damn things must have hopped off like rabbits . . ." Murphy slapped his hat against his pants leg and put it on, swinging his eyes around again. "Can't see 'em . . ."

"I'll get the fire going and make some coffee," Midge said, "while you find them."

Murphy nodded, fetched a piece of rope from the wagon, and started walking out in circles around the camp. He cut their tracks leading east on his second circuit—shuffle-stepping tracks because they'd had to short-step in the hobbles. They had worked down a moist but not flowing streambed, following the greener grass near and on the edges, and he found them a quarter of a mile down the curving bed, hidden in a low swale. They snorted when they saw him coming and one of them turned to him, but the other mule actually made three or four hops to get away from him.

"Damn mules." But he smiled. The mule looked ridiculous hopping, like a great gray rabbit. But it made twenty yards or so down the creekbed, then climbed up the edge, and he had to trot to catch up to it. When he did, it turned easily enough and let him tie the rope to its halter. Murphy had turned to get the other mule when he saw the movement.

At first he wasn't sure he'd seen it—some small movement two or three hundred yards down the streambed where it opened out into a deeper, wider gully. But old habits die hard, and he froze, his hand moving to his hip. His fingers splayed against the empty cloth where the Smith would have been.

No gun. Always there had been a gun there and now it was gone. He took half a breath, held it, then let it out slowly, staring at the spot where he had last seen the movement, or thought he had seen it.

For moments—long moments—he saw nothing. Then, with startling suddenness, a floppy hat appeared: an old beat-up brown floppy hat. Beneath the hat, rising from the gully, came a broad, flat face. An old face, surrounded by hanging clotted strands of gray hair. As the head rose magically from the ground, it was followed by a grubby red flannel shirt, then a pony's head, and finally the whole figure was there—an old Indian riding a pony that looked so ancient it seemed to be held together by the rope cinch holding the piece of leather being used for a saddle. The horse was pulling a *travois*, two poles leading back to a pole platform that skidded and bounced along; and when the horse turned sideways a bit Murphy saw that there was a passenger on the travois. A woman who seemed to be as old as the man riding the pony sat, facing backwards, holding the poles. Two braids hung down to her sides and she was wearing an old cavalry jacket, the blue wool frayed and worn.

Murphy relaxed and watched them move toward him. There were no other Indians and Murphy couldn't see a weapon. The old man let the pony make its own way up the streambed—the pony had seen the mules and picked up the pace a bit, thinking it was the place to stop—and Murphy took a moment to attach the rope to the mules, one end to each mule. Then he detached the hobbles and put them around his shoulders. The mules snuffled and whickered to the pony and poked their ears forward but held steady for all of that, and when the pony was close it stopped and the old man smiled.

"Hello, my friend," the old man said, "we smelled your coffee."

Some nose, Murphy thought.

"It smells like very good coffee."

Well, hell, Murphy thought—we have lots of coffee. "Why don't you join us for some of it?"

The old man shrugged. "We have to ride for the mountains today to make the places of grass where the elk spend the summertime. But we can make time for coffee if you wish it. Tell me, would it be possible that you have some bacon to go with the coffee? It has been a long time since my woman has had any bacon fat and she needs the fat to stay round and warm at night." He spoke in a singing sound, the words like water over rocks, and Murphy couldn't help but widen his smile. "No, we haven't got any bacon. But there might be some ham."

"Ham fat is the same as bacon fat. It all helps to make women round."

"Yes, it does." Murphy turned and pulled at the mules and they followed him easily—always a surprise.

Midge watched him approach the camp, her eyes widening when she saw the Indian pony bringing the elderly couple.

"I brought company," Murphy said, tying the mules to the wagon. "For breakfast."

"I see." Midge stood and wiped her hands on her dress front, forgetting that she wasn't wearing an apron.

Murphy's eyes smiled. "He wants some bacon fat to keep his wife round. I told him we didn't have any but that you might come up with some ham. While you're at it, maybe you'd better eat some ham yourself. I think you could stand to be a little rounder."

"You do, do you?"

The Indian stopped his pony and brought his right leg over to slip to the ground. The movement was as light as that of a young man, though the man was obviously ancient. The woman remained sitting on the travois, her back to all of them, staring out across the grass to the east.

"You have a good woman there," the old man said to Murphy, and then, as if having heard their conversation, "except that she is too thin. Sometimes they will get more round as time goes by, but that is not always the case. That coffee smells better close than it did far. Where is the ham?"

He stopped talking and stood, staring at the coffeepot

next to the fire. His woman hadn't moved from the travois, hadn't turned her head.

Midge turned to look at Murphy, a question in her eyes, and he nodded. She went to the wagon and found two extra cups, brought them back to the fire and poured them full of coffee. Murphy took them and handed them to the old man, who nodded gratefully and drank both cups down, slurping loudly and smacking his lips.

Murphy stared at him. The coffee was scalding hot, lead hot, and it didn't seem to bother the old man at all.

"Thank you. That is good coffee. For my woman, it would be nice if you had some of the white sweet powder. She would be happy and I need to keep her happy." Murphy took the cups and handed them to Midge, who found some sugar in a feed sack in the wagon and put a spoonful into a cup.

"She likes it when there are many measures of the white sweet powder," the old man corrected. Midge put in two and looked up; he waited . . . she put two more in and then put the spoon back. She poured the coffee on the sugar in the cup, stirred the thick potion, and handed it to the old man, who took it at once to the woman on the travois. She took it almost daintily, sipping it with much lip sound, and he turned back to Murphy and Midge. "Why is it that you ride north?"

Murphy was startled at the question, then remembered the tracks cut in the grass that led south in back of the wagon. The old man saw everything.

"We are going to look for land and some cattle . . ."

The old man nodded thoughtfully, thinking. After a moment he shrugged. "It is not my place to say, but you do not look like a man who would raise cattle. You look like a man who has done other things. One of those white men who hunt men."

"You're right," Murphy said. "It's not your place to say."

The Indian shrugged again and turned to the woman. He said nothing but the woman suddenly wriggled to the side of the travois, moved to the wagon, pushed Midge aside, and began to rummage through the packed goods. It almost seemed she knew where things were. In seconds she had the pot and the ham out, had pulled a greasy knife from somewhere beneath her cavalry coat, and had cut slices which she threw in the pot. From another pocket she found a double handful of some beans, which she added, and took water from the barrel in the wagon to pour on top.

All of this seemed to occur in seconds, while Murphy watched and Midge stood with her mouth half open and one hand raised in a half-hearted protest. When the old lady had the pot nestled in the coals, she worked dry wood around it to make more flame and stood to smile at Midge with a mouth that seemed to have only one usable tooth, sticking up from the bottom middle of her mouth.

"My woman is good at cooking," the old man said. "Maybe it is that she can help your woman to get round."

Murphy sighed, resigned, and grinned at the fire in Midge's eyes. He could tell she didn't want anybody messing with her fire or food or wagon. The pot had to cook now, the beans, and he didn't see how he could get rid of the old man. He had wanted to get an early start and now they would have to wait for the food.

He found the grain in the wagon and gave some to the mules, then handed the sack to the old man. It was likely the pony had never had grain—God knew what it would do with some oats in it—but the Indian fed it a sensible double handful. Any more might have bloated it, and the pony ate it gratefully before turning back to its grazing, dragging the now empty travois behind it.

"It is too bad we are not traveling north," the old man said, squatting near the fire. "We could travel together . . ."

Murphy saw Midge blanch at the thought and shook his head. "We are not ready to travel with anybody else."

"I have been north," the old man said suddenly. "Where do you plan to go?"

"We're looking for good grass."

The old man thought a moment, then smiled across the fire at his woman, who sat near the pot waiting for the beans and ham. She sat flat-legged, her legs stretched out to the front, stirring the beans now and then with a stick. "Where was that grass, that good grass that came up to the pony's belly? Where was that?"

She said nothing, didn't look at him, gave no indication she'd even heard him, but in a moment he nodded and looked at Murphy.

"My woman says it was out of that place the white men call Casper, up along the mountains. A few days out of that place, there is a canyon that leads to a meadow where there is sweet grass and good water. That might be the place you wish to find."

Murphy kneeled next to the old man. Midge handed him a cup of coffee and he sipped it. The mules stretched against their ropes and grabbed for tufts of grass. "You say meadow—about how big would that meadow be?"

"I do not know how to measure as white men measure. But for riding it would take half of one morning to ride across it the short way and a whole morning to ride the long way. There is a stream that moves through it and some of those small sweet fish in the stream."

"It sounds beautiful," Midge said suddenly. "Really beautiful."

No, Murphy thought—it sounds more than beautiful. It sounds like home.

CHAPTER 3

CASPER was a raw sea of mud.

The old Indian and his woman had moved on three days earlier, and Murphy and Midge had traveled in sunshine and clear skies for two of those days. On the third one, the rain started. They had put on their slickers and kept riding, but soon the rain worked under them and into them and they were soaked through. Worse, the twin-rutted trail that passed for a road turned into a quagmire and one of the mules threw a shoe. Murphy wanted to stop but he had to get to the smithy in Casper and get a new shoe before the mule drew up lame. They had continued all night in the rain and found Casper just after dawn.

They smelled it before they saw it. The rain had flooded all the outhouses in back of the buildings and turned the alleys into a sewer.

The mules slathered onto the main street with their legs sucking at each step, humping and heaving to pull the wagon down the crowded street. Cowboys, brought to town by the rain that kept them from working, were looking for early drinks and early women and the tradesmen were eager to oblige.

Murphy had a moment of gratitude that he was no longer a lawman—by tonight whoever ran the law in Casper was going to have his hands full. The cowboys would be drunk by noon and piss-mean by dark; they would be waiting to fight anything that moved by mid-night. Rain was always bad.

The bed of the wagon dragged and added to the load and Murphy jumped off and held the reins to the side to get his weight off the wagon.

"It was a mistake to come into town . . ." He swore at the mules and jerked the lines. Near the end of the single street there was a livery, and he sawed and yelled the mules to the large central door.

A short, round man with a red face and shoulders like a dwarf stood in the doorway. He spit a gray stream of tobacco juice into the mud and smiled with yellow teeth. "Muddy enough for you?" He moved aside as Murphy jerked the mules into the livery, the wagon with them.

"I need a couple of stalls and somebody who can shoe a mule," Murphy said, wiping the mud from his boots. The mud was halfway to his waist and he finally gave up.

"Costs fifty cents a day," the livery man said, "but I give you oats for that. Half a quart a day. I'll get the smithy over here to fix the shoe, but that'll cost a dollar. Another quarter to leave the wagon here." He frowned and spit, scratching his chin. "Comes to a dollar and six bits. In advance."

Murphy paid him. "Is there a hotel here that isn't loaded with bugs?"

Another scratch. "The onliest one in town be the Hart place. Not rightly a hotel, but he's got some rooms and if you get a clean one it ain't too buggy. It's across the street and up to the end."

Murphy lifted Midge down and grabbed the bedrolls and they went to the door. There were no boardwalks in Casper and Midge held her skirts up, but Murphy laughed and easily picked her up. He crossed the street, weaving through horses and two more wagons fighting the mud. At the end of the street was a rough-sawn, two-story frame house—a drunken cowboy pointed it out as the Hart place—and Murphy carried Midge until he could set her down on the plank porch.

There wasn't a Hart. The place was run by a thin, unsmiling woman named Parker, and she had a room on the top floor that was surprisingly clean. It was an unpainted wooden room with one window, but it held a brass bed and the window had a curtain and shade, and there was a dresser with a porcelain pitcher and bowl to wash in—all for only fifty cents a night, plus a nickel for clean towels.

Midge grabbed the pitcher of water as soon as the door closed. "I've got a lot of trail in my hair," she said, leaning over the bowl and pouring water into her hair with the pitcher. "You check on the smithy, and bring the sleeping gear back up when you come and we'll dry it out."

Murphy nodded silently, watching her in quiet wonder. He'd done things for himself all his life and it seemed strange to have somebody willing to take over. To have his life mixed with the life of somebody else. All of this seemed strange to him.

He left her soaping her hair and went back into the street, into the mud and noise. It didn't seem possible that Casper would have so many people—when he was the law in Cincherville it seemed that the town was always studying different ways to die—and he stopped for a bit on the front porch to watch it. After a moment he realized that many of the men were repeats: they'd go from a store on one side of the street to a harness shop on the other side, then across to a saloon. And there seemed to be a saloon for every man on the street. Casper was a rough, dirty town. Over two of the saloons he saw cribs with women in the windows calling down to the cowboys, and some of the men would go up outside stairways to take advantage of them.

Murphy snorted. Most of them would get what the miners called the pony drip, and they knew they would but it didn't seem to slow them down much. He ignored the noise and looked northwest at the sky and was gratified to see some blue patches. What was it old Colonel who ran the livery in Cincherville used to say? Oh, yeah, if there was enough blue to make a Dutchman's pants it would clear off and warm up. He smiled to himself. How the hell much material did it take to make a Dutchman's pants? Well, if it cleared it would dry fast and he didn't want to stay in Casper any longer than absolutely necessary. Just long enough to buy some gear and head north, looking for the meadow the old Indian had spoken of, the sweet grass meadow.

He stepped down into the mud—which was like lowering himself into quicksand—and made his way back to the livery. The livery manager was as good as his word, and the smithy was there putting a shoe on the mule while the livery man held his bridle. The smithy was a coarse, muscled man covered with hair, his cheek full of tobacco. Just as Murphy walked up he stood away from the mule, threw the cold shoe and his hammer on the ground, and swore loudly, staring at the mule's head.

"Goddam, I hate a mule. My mother always told me I'd hate a mule and goddam I hate a mule. They'll wait and stick you. They'll wait and think and stick you when you don't expect it. Goddam I hate a mule."

Murphy smiled. "What's he doing to you?"

"Son of a bitch waits until I start to nail the shoe then he leans on me. Starts light and brings the weight down more and more until it's like to bust my goddam leg. Goddam I hate a mule."

Murphy stepped forward and took the halter from the livery man. "Go ahead, do it again, and I'll ear him when he comes over." The smithy raised the mule's left front leg again—the mule gave his foot easily enough— and took the foot on his leg, pushing his shoulder up into the mule's side. As soon as he put the shoe against the hoof the mule started to lean. Murphy pulled the mule's ear down and bit the end of it and the lean stopped. He bit a little harder and the mule shifted his weight off the smithy and stood calmly on his other three legs while the smithy nailed the shoe and cut and bent the nails. When he was done he stood and spit and held his hand out for Murphy's dollar.

"He throws that new shoe and you bring him back for a free one. Whoever shoed it last time didn't crimp them nails over right and they worked out."

Murphy nodded. It had probably been one of the miners at the McClintock mine outside Cincherville, where Murphy bought the mules. Another place, another life.

"Where's a good store for outfitting?" He asked the livery man when the smithy was gone and the mule was back in the stall next to its teammate. "I need working tools and supplies."

"For mining?" The livery man snorted. "Hell, there ain't no mines left around here."

No, Murphy thought, not mining. For farming. For ranching. For dirt. "Just general supplies."

"That'd be over to Tucker's, across the street. Tucker will skin you if he can but he don't lie and his stuff don't break. The other dry goods place is some cheaper, but they sell bad—I ain't ever bought a fork handle that didn't break from Sutler's—so it's best to go to Tucker and pay a little more."

Murphy thanked him and started across the street. He had taken three or four steps toward the other side of the street when some movement caught his eye and he looked off to the right to see a child, a small boy, stepping off a board that crossed between two buildings. The boy fell sideways into the street, and other than getting covered with mud that should have been it.

But at that moment, with his head turned, Murphy felt and heard horses coming fast on his left, and he turned to see a line abreast of mud-covered horses coming down the street through the mud at a slathering, flying, splattering run. In that split second Murphy's eyes, trained to respond to split-second movements, saw two things. First, the horses were not ridden by cowhands. The men on the horses were carrying guns—some of them several handguns—that cowboys wouldn't carry, rifles in well-oiled scabbards. Working cowboys carried one gun, if that, a work gun, usually a rusted old Colts-patent thumb-buster. These men were carrying enough guns for a small army. That came into Murphy's sight instantly. He always saw guns instantly.

And the second thing to hit him was that the riders—he sensed seven or eight men, there was no time to count—were not going to stop before they ran over the small boy.

All in a second, or half a second, he saw the riders thundering down the muddy street, the guns at their waists and in the scabbards beneath their legs, the boy fallen in the mud, up on one arm trying to rise, his face turned away from the oncoming horses. All of it was in his eyes and on his mind, and he acted without thinking.

He stepped forward one large step and put himself in front of the horses. In the same motion one hand swept his hat off his head and slapped it across the face of the horse closest to hitting the boy. His other hand swung down, caught the boy by the back of his shirt, tore him from the mud, and threw him back against the wall of the livery.

Everything happened and was over in a second, but his weight carried him forward and his feet couldn't catch up. He was falling and couldn't stop it, and as he fell, he saw that the horse he had slapped had shied sideways so hard that it too was going down and the man who had been riding it—Murphy got a glimpse of a bearded, snarling face—kicked loose from his stirrups and came cartwheeling over his horse's head.

Then it was all a swirling, flopping mess of mud and falling horses as the one horse hit another and tripped it and that one caught another. The horse's head slammed down not four inches from Murphy's face, and he jerked back to avoid the animal's flailing hooves as it tried to get up.

The boy had slammed hard against the wall, and Murphy rolled to his feet—covered with mud from one end to the other—to check on the boy, and he actually took a step before the voice stopped him

"Right there, mister. Stop and turn right there."

The voice was low and guttural, and Murphy turned slowly to find himself facing the bearded man who was on his feet and had a Colt's revolver aimed at Murphy's stomach. Murphy felt his gut tighten. His old nightmare was there, the dream of a man shooting him in the belly while Murphy watches the bullet leave the barrel of the gun and travel slowly toward him, watches the bullet hit his stomach and punch dust from his shirt . . .

Murphy shook the thoughts away. "I'm not carrying a gun," he said. He needed time. Time to settle the man, time to talk the gun down so he could take him.

"I'm not sure if that matters—you having a gun or not. You've caused me some kind of trouble here and generally I kill people who cause me trouble."

He was a thin man, covered with a fur coat that looked to weigh a hundred pounds. He had flat eyes, snake eyes, eyes that looked cold.

Murphy said nothing. The talking was done. If the man was talking he probably wouldn't shoot. At least not right away. Now he had to move closer. The other horses were getting to their feet, the other men swearing and jerking their mounts around. Out of the corner of his eye he saw the boy stand and start moving away down the livery wall. He had to get closer to the man, get inside a range where he could get his hands on him before the other seven men—he could count them now—could move in on him.

Murphy took a step sidways and one forward, pulling his feet as if stuck in the mud and trying to get them loose. The man with the pistol watched him, but the pistol didn't follow him, and as the second step brought him forward, Murphy moved.

His left arm clubbed the handgun down and away and his right fist slammed straight-line into the man's face. He aimed for a point about half a foot in back of the man's head, and the force of the blow had all the weight of Murphy's frame in back of it. The gunman was unconscious before his head moved half an inch, and Murphy scooped the Colt's from his hand in an easy motion, changed it to his right hand as the man started to fall, wheeled the man and held him as a shield, and aimed the gun at the other seven men.

"I don't want this to go any further," he said evenly. "Let's just keep it sensible."

There was some movement, men's hands drifted to guns. They were hard men. Murphy could see that now. Rock men. Ugly men. But they saw the steady barrel of the Colt's and knew that he would use it and their hands held.

"You know who that is?" One of them pointed to the unconscious man Murphy held. "You put Darrin Teason down."

Murphy didn't know the name but it didn't matter. He knew the type. Long riders, riders who took what they wanted when they wanted it. They hadn't come to Cincherville when he was the law because there wasn't anything in Cincherville to draw them and because he would have made it too expensive for their type to try. But Murphy wasn't law anymore, and he wasn't being paid to stop them.

"I don't want any trouble," he said.

"Well you've got some, Mister."

"I don't think so," a new voice boomed in. Murphy turned to see a large fat man standing at the corner of the livery. On his chest, wired to his vest, was a badge, and in his arms, loosely aimed at all seven of the men, he held a double twelve.

"Name's Hiram," he said, cocking both hammers on the twelve-gauge. "Ain't you Murphy, used to be the law in Cincherville?"

Murphy nodded. "I'm just passing through. Sorry to cause trouble here."

"Ain't no trouble, no trouble at all." Hiram swung the barrel of the shotgun back and forth and spit another stream of tobacco juice. "You boys shuck all them guns—all of 'em—and throw 'em over here by the livery wall." There was some grumbling and a moment's hesitation and Hiram added, "If you don't, I'm going to pick one of you and use a load of double-ought to make you into two pieces."

It was clear from his voice that he meant it, and in a moment there was a pile of firearms—rifles and handguns—against the livery wall.

"That'll be good. Now come and pick up your man and move on out of town." He pointed at the still unconscious man Murphy was holding up. Murphy let him drop into the mud and two of the riders picked him up and dragged him to his horse, which had regained its feet. They threw him up in the saddle and two of the men mounted and rode alongside him to hold him in. His head was rolling but he was starting to come out of it.

"What about our guns?" one of them called back as the horses worked through the mud.

"I'm adding them to my collection," Hiram called. "You can get new somewheres else. Just don't come back here." He spit again but the barrel stayed on the backs of the riders.

"I want to thank you for stepping in like that," Murphy said, letting the Colt's drop and taking the tension out of his shoulders. "I'm not sure I could have handled them."

"Well, you was doing all right when I got here. That one was slobbering like you hit him with a shovel."

"Just luck. I got inside his gun or he would have had me."

They stood, watching them men ride out the end of Casper, and Murphy hoped they would keep riding, hoped that his luck would continue to hold until he could change, could be with Midge and live enough to not have to get inside a gun facing him. He hoped that he could hope enough to make it happen; but a pocket in his mind held back from the hope, a small, dark pocket of something he didn't understand, and the hairs on the back of his neck tightened as he watched the men ride out of town.

CHAPTER 4

FOUR days north of Casper, Murphy and Midge gave up on the sweet grass canyon the old Indian had told them about.

"I think we ought to head up into Montana like we thought at first," Murphy said when they stopped for the day near a small creek that carved mud across the prairie

They had bought some horses before leaving Casper; now Murphy climbed stiffly off the seat and went back to loosen the bell mare they had tied to the rear of the wagon so that the rest of the horses would follow. She whickered and nuzzled him, and he wondered why horses would like a man and mules wouldn't. He put hobbles on her and turned her loose. The rest of the horses would move away a bit but they'd stay close to her and follow when Murphy caught her up and tied her to the wagon next morning.

Murphy thought about how the town marshall had befriended Midge and him and taken them under his wing after the incident with the riders.

"Them sonsabitches mought just lay for you when you leave," Hiram had said, spitting. He seemed to spit with every ten words, and Murphy noticed that Midge had to turn away or look at the sky when he spit. "Best you lay over here a day or two and let them ride on a ways . . ."

So Murphy had told him what they wanted, to start a

27

small ranch where they could live peacefully, and it was no surprise to Murphy that Hiram readily agreed.

"Goddam badge ain't nothing but a target," he'd grumbled. "But was I you, I wouldn't mess with cows. Cows ain't nothing but trouble, always getting botworms and the goddam scours. I hate cows. Go six and a half miles out of my way to shoot a cow. No sir, what you want to do is raise horses. You worm 'em once a year with tobacco and sell them green as willow to the army for remounts and let the bluebellies get stomped. You got a market there that will last a long time and less trouble to boot. Let me know if you want to do horses. I know a stock broker which ain't too dishonest."

Midge and Murphy had talked it over that night in the boarding house—they couldn't sleep because a drummer in the next room kept wheezing and coughing, and the thin walls did nothing to reduce the sound—and decided Hiram was right. Neither of them knew anything about raising cattle, and Murphy had at least a running acquaintance with horses. The next morning they'd gone to see Hiram again, and true to his word he'd introduced them to a horse trader.

The man looked and acted—according to Midge—just like a weasel that was about to take all your chickens. He was thin, with a narrow face and long teeth and a vest so filthy from wiping his hands on it, so covered with dirt and manure and stink, that it would have stood without him. But he had some good horses—even Murphy could tell that when he saw them—in a pen outside of town, and he was willing to dicker.

"They's two studs and twenty-seven brood mares and two geldings," said the trader, whose name was Whacker, or at least that's what he said. "They's good stock, none of 'em over four years old, too good for the army just to take as remounts. That's why I still got 'em." He picked his nose and wiped it on his vest. "I figger they's worth at least sixty a head."

"That's crazy," Hiram said, spitting. Midge turned nearly green, what with the broker and his nose, Hiram and his spit. "They ain't gold, just horses. And what the hell does he do with geldings? He can't breed them to nothing."

"He's got to ride, don't he? All right, fifty-five a head and that's bottom."

"Well, if that's bottom you'll just have to eat the damn things. They ain't worth a dime over fifty and then only if you'll throw in a saddle for the lady and a bell mare to keep them in line on a drive," Hiram said, turning away, gesturing Midge and Murphy to follow him. Before they'd gone four paces Whacker called to them.

"You can't get doodlum for fifty dollars a head and you know it, Hiram. Not good horses. My rock bottom is fifty-five and a bell mare and a saddle. But that's it and I don't care if you walk to death."

"Done!" Hiram said, and Murphy realized he and Midge had spent most of their money—from the gold Wangsu's widow had given them in Cincherville when he found the men who killed her husband—and they hadn't said a word. They went to the bank, converted the gold bar into cash, paid for the horses, and took Hiram out for a steak dinner at a café, which Midge liked because she didn't have to cook.

"I have just one question," Midge asked, when they had finished dinner and eaten pie. "How did you know I didn't have a saddle?"

Hiram looked for a place to spit, couldn't find one, and swallowed. "Didn't. But you always ask for more than you expect when you deal with a horse trader, and

I just threw the saddle in at the last there. I never figured he'd do it. Worked out all right, didn't it?"

And two days later, after spending most of the rest of their money on supplies that heaped the wagon over their heads, they left Casper and started the slow ride northwest up along the front of the mountains.

The peaks rose to their left, as they had continuously for the past two weeks. The weather had held good for them after the rain outside of Casper, and they had honeymoon-rolled the wagon through miles and miles of new prairie flowers brought by the rain. They could not have paid for better traveling, but they had not seen the "two tall rock leg mountains" the Indian had said marked the canyon, and they had not found any other kind of sweet grass valley.

"We'll start angling north tomorrow and maybe try to get up to Billings." Murphy eased the weight of the Smith on his hip. He'd worn the gun since the fracas in Casper and kept a rifle under the wagon seat, but they hadn't seen any trace of the riders and he was sick of the four pounds of steel on his hip all day. He took it off now, wrapping the belt around the holster, and thought again of the valley they sought.

To be sure, Murphy had never really thought it existed. He had talked to many Indians and listened to many more when he was in the army, when he was young and fresh out of the east. He had never had to fight them—as most of the army had never had to fight them—but he knew enough from listening to them to understand that they didn't use the same rules when describing something.

A place could be one thing and they could make it into anything else they wanted, or you wanted. If they thought you wanted a sweet grass valley, they would tell you about one even if there wasn't one, because that is what you wanted to hear and they wanted you to be happy. He could never figure why they were so nice to whites when the whites spent most of their time treating them like dirt.

He knew a soldier once who checked the sights on his Springfield by shooting at an Indian woman a hundred yards away, and when the rifle threw low and hit the woman in the leg—nearly taking the leg off and dropping her—he calmly adjusted the sight and shot her again, killing her, and said nothing except to complain about his rifle throwing low.

And still the Indians were good to the whites. Good until they were pushed so hard, hurt so hard, killed so hard that they could do nothing but fight; and then everybody screamed about the "blood-thirsty savages" and fought to destroy them.

But they did have some different ideas about places and times. When the old man said to ride a few days along the mountains from Casper it might have meant a couple of weeks. Might have. But it also depended on what the old man thought the white man was riding. If he thought the white man rode fast horses, the canyon might be up to a hundred miles north. And with Murphy and Midge waddling along in a mule-drawn wagon, pulling a bell mare and forty horses at twelve or fifteen miles a day, it could take many days.

If there was a canyon in the first place. Murphy had wanted there to be one, but he finally now admitted to himself that it was probably a dream and they were just chasing hope.

They set camp quickly. By now they were old hands at it, and Murphy was having trouble remembering what it was like before, in town. Midge jumped lightly down—

she amazed him with her strength; she never seemed to tire—and found stones for a fire pit. He loosened the mules and held them on a long rope while they rolled the harness sweat off and shook down. Then he watered them and grained them and tied them to the ring in the front of the wagon tongue, still with a long rope—putting them on a picket now instead of a hobbles—and found wood for a fire.

In minutes they had a fire going, and he used a metal bucket they'd bought in Casper along with the small mountain of other dry goods they thought they'd need to start a ranch, to get water from a small stream nearby. The spring runoff was still fresh from the winter snows and spring rains (the mountains were white halfway down their sides though it was close to June) and the prairie was a spider web of creeks and rivulets.

Murphy put coffee water in the blackened pot, which he nestled in the coals against the flames. Then he took half a handful of Arbuckle coffee beans, wrapped them in a piece of ticking, and smashed them against a rock, using the flat edge of a single-bladed axe. When the beans were pulverized he threw them in the heating water and tied a tarp to the side of the wagon. When it was secured he pulled it out to the side to make an angled-down roof—it kept the morning mist off their blankets even if it didn't rain—spread their bed beneath it, and turned to see that Midge hd a pot of stew left over from the previous night nearly hot enough to eat.

"Maybe," he said, stretching, "we don't ever have to settle. We're getting so good at traveling we could just keep going. Head north in spring and move south in fall. Like the buffalo used to do."

"Speak for yourself," Midge answered. She snaked the pot off the fire and tipped the lid back. Steam poured off and Murphy instantly began to salivate. "I'm ready to settle in someplace," she said. She looked east across the prairie. "It must have been something to see, though—the buffalo. Just a few years ago—think of it, Al—just a few years ago and you couldn't see across their backs. They say it would take a week for a herd to pass you, trotting day and night."

For a moment they stood in silence, the fire at their feet, looking across the grass, thinking of it. Then she sighed and said, "I love you."

He touched her hair where the evening light hit it, the small hairs in front of her ear, over her temple. "I can't believe how this works," he said quietly. "How looking at buffalo that aren't there makes us think this way but it does. It's like all the flowers, all the air, all the sky and land and all of it is part of loving each other . . ."

They sat on the edge of the bedroll together and ate in silence, still taken by the fullness of it. And when they were done and the plates cleaned and rinsed in the stream, they slid into the blankets and let that be part of it as well.

He saw them at first light, when he stood from the fire to take a sip of coffee.

Dawn snaked across the prairie from the east and front-lighted the whole mountain range to the west, and in the new light, the flat light, he saw eight or ten miles ahead two stone pillars. At first he thought he was imagining them, and he pointed them out to Midge.

"There, to the left and ahead. What do you see?"

She squinted and then smiled, nodding. "I see them. Do you suppose that's what he was talking about?"

"I don't know. It might be. We must have lost them in

the evening light yesterday. But we're sure going to find out." Only a couple of days off, he thought—that's not so bad. A rider on a horse would have made it in two or three days, taking it easy on a horse, so the old man wasn't that far off. Make it between forty and sixty miles or so. If it was the right place. If.

He couldn't keep from becoming excited and the excitement transmitted itself to the animals. The mules snorted and jumped, and he pulled and shoved them roughly into place when he finally had them harnessed. The jenny took a halfhearted cut at him and he slapped her lightly across the side of her head just to let her know she wasn't getting away with it, but he knew she wasn't serious. She hadn't even bared her teeth.

Midge packed everything into the wagon and was done when he walked back with the bell mare. Most of the grazing horses ignored him, but he knew they would follow when he started out.

He climbed into the seat and took the lines from Midge, slapped them lightly across the rumps of the mules, and they were moving as they had moved for two weeks, day after day. But this day was different.

He held them off to the left. After half a mile he felt Midge's hand on his arm, gripping it, holding it, and when he turned she was watching the two stone pillars, pulling at them with her eyes. He smiled and patted her hand with his, but she didn't let go. Not then and not the whole time he drove the mules slowly, trying hard to not whip them into a run.

All morning they rode, the wagon rocking as it crossed each creek, the bell mare plodding along behind, the thirty other horses strung out in a fat line, following in the dust, and not once did Midge take her hand from Murphy's arm.

CHAPTER 5

THEY ran into a deep streambed, and they had to swing sideways and ride east for almost four miles to find a way across before they could work their way back to their original trail, and that cut into daylight. Just at dark they found themselves at the base of the pillars—which were actually two buttes about a mile apart but seeming taller than they were because they were so narrow at the top.

A stream, wide and with a rocky bottom, wound its way out between the buttes, and both banks were strung with cottonwoods. They pulled the wagon into a small grassy area near the stream and set up camp, all in silence. They wanted to get into the canyon and see it, finally see it, but they had to wait until morning.

They made a fire, had sandwiches, and went to bed as soon as it was dark, forcing sleep and still largely not talking. It was not a strained silence so much as a waiting silence. Murphy knew that it, the silence, was just that they were hoping.

All the years in Cincherville, all the puking drunks and bar fights and Midge cooking for people, working her hands raw until midnight, all the broken promises and dreams, and they still couldn't believe they might have found their dream. Their place.

So they didn't talk and they pretended to sleep until hard dark came when they both dozed, wrapped in each other's arms against the night coolness sweeping down the canyon between the two buttes.

At first light, when the sky was just turning gray out across the prairie, Murphy rolled out and harnessed the mules. They didn't light a fire, didn't wait for coffee, but tied the bell mare on and broke camp cold and met dawn riding into the canyon.

For a mile it was still nearly dark and they wound through the cottonwoods along the stream, letting the mules make their own way. Once Murphy had to get off and manhandle a dead tree that had fallen across in front of the them.

And just when the sun brought full light, splashed gold through the opening between the buttes, just then the wagon and mules broke out of the cottonwoods into the open.

"Ohhhh . . ." Midge gasped. "Oh, Al, look at it!"

The valley swept up before them. Murphy couldn't be sure but it looked to be seven or eight miles long, moving back in between the buttes in a gentle, shallow curve. It was at least three quarters of a mile across here, at the narrow point, and opened into a huge, flat plain that seemed to be cupped by mountains.

And the old Indian had been right. It was lush green with new summer grass. Caught in the first growth, the grass had shot up until it was close to the bellies on the mules and horses, and it was so green it almost hurt their eyes. Once, in the Tenderloin when he was a boy and trying to stay alive with his mother, she had been drunk, talking of Ireland, of "the dear old Emerald Isle," and he had listened to her speak of the lush green of her old home for a whole night until she became too drunk to talk.

Somehow the green had stuck in his mind and he

thought of it now, thought this must be how Ireland looks. But he didn't speak, in a way couldn't speak. The valley entranced him. It was like the first time he had seen Midge. Not at work in the café, but the first time he saw her in bed with no clothes on—he almost couldn't touch her, couldn't speak because he thought he would break what was between them the way he broke so many other things in his life. The way he broke his life.

Now it was the same. He didn't think but felt that if he spoke, if he made a single sound, it would all shatter like a painting on a window he had seen in a church. A word, a single sound from him, would ruin it.

The grass waved slowly in the morning breeze that the warming temperature drew up the valley. A quarter of a mile ahead of them a small herd of antelope—not over ten of them—stopped grazing to watch them without fear, and still further they saw the dark brown blotches of buffalo moving slowly as they sought the tender shoots of young grass. Murphy couldn't be sure, but there seemed to be twenty or more of them.

The stream they had followed wound gently down through the rough middle of the valley, except at one point where it moved off to the right, close to the canyon wall. Here it had found or carved a depression and made a small pond of perhaps an acre and a half, and cottonwoods and some white pines had set up residence around the pond, making a natural shaded park with a canyon wall at its back.

It was a perfect place, the perfect place for a cabin. For a home. Murphy slapped the mules with the reins and they made for the pond as if drawn by a string. The bell mare followed, still tied to the wagon, but the rest of the horses—as if sensing this was where they were going to stop—spread out and began to graze. The bell mare felt left out and whickered to them, but they ignored her.

It took only half an hour to get to the pond. Ducks lifted from the water as the wagon approached, wheeling and catching the light from the morning sun so their wings flashed silver as they flew low further up the canyon. There must be another pond up there, Murphy thought, or a wide place in the stream. They'd have to saddle a couple of the horses and ride up the valley and see what was there. They'd have to do that and they'd have to settle in and they'd have to build a cabin and get some firewood cut. No, they'd have to build a corral and some kind of shelter for the stock. No, early in the year like this they'd have to get some ground dug up for a kitchen garden. No. They'd have to . . . his mind reeled with it. They'd have to do everything he'd never done before. They'd have to live.

"Do you think we can?" Midge whispered, as if reading his mind. "Do you really think we can do this?"

Murphy studied the canyon walls, the blue sky, the green grass out before them and sighed. "The way I see it, we don't have any choice. This is all we have left. We spent some time getting here, one thing and another, and I'm going to give it one hell of a shot—make it or not."

The mules stopped when they came into the shade of the cottonwoods, and Murphy jumped down and ran around the wagon before Midge could get down so that he was waiting for her.

"Your arm, ma'am?" he said, smiling.

"Why, of course," she answered. "Of course, my young gentleman."

He lifted her easily down and held her for a moment.

Some hair had come loose from the leather tie she held it back with, and he used a finger to push it away from her temple.

"Welcome home," he said to her.

"And it's good to be here," she said. "It's good to be home."

The mules suddenly stomped their impatience. They had been two weeks in harness day on day, except for the brief stop in Casper; and if this was where they were going to stop, by God, so be it and enough of this foolishness.

Murphy found a place under some cottonwoods, away from the pond enough to let the breeze carry the mosquitos off—they were starting to gather as the morning sun warmed the earth—and pulled the wagon in. They'd have to live under the wagon and tarp until he got a shelter up, and he wanted it in the right place.

Midge started a fire—they had broken camp cold and both wanted coffee and some breakfast, and Murphy unharnessed the mules and then stopped.

Just stopped. He was standing at the front end of the mules—they still had the collars on—and he held one harness in his hands and the other draped over a tree limb and he stopped. Everything in him stopped, all his thinking stopped, and he had a momentary sense of raw panic.

"Midge," he said quietly, "Midge, I don't know if I can do this."

"Do what?" She had filled the pot at the pond and was by the fire, moving it into position in the flames.

He shrugged helplessly. "All of it, any of it. Jesus, Midge, I'm thirty-two years old, and all I've ever done is jail drunks or suck knuckles for forty a month. I don't know the first thing about ranching or raising horses or building anything . . ." He trailed off, flopping a line from the harness against his leg aimlessly, knocking out little spurts of dust.

Midge stood and wiped her hands on her dress and walked up to him, smiling gently. She took the harness from him and hung it over another tree limb. "The leather's drying out," she said. "I'll give you some lard and you work it in to keep it from cracking . . ."

"Midge . . ."

"Oh, hell, Al," she said, wheeling suddenly with some anger in her eyes. "You act like we had a choice, like it mattered. Can't you see, we're all we need? How hard can it be to do this? There are men out here who can't pour piss out of a boot with the instructions written on the heel and they're raising cattle, horses—living. If they can do it, we can do it. We're willing to work and we can do it. Now, let's set to coffee and then get to work."

Murphy stared at her while she took four steps back to the rear of the wagon and got beans to break for coffee. She handed him the handful of beans and the cloth and axe and turned back to the fire to add more wood—still without speaking, though there was color in her cheeks—and Murphy smashed the beans against a rock in silence. And they stayed in silence until the coffee was done and they had filled two cups, the steam working up around their faces as they sipped, the sun well up over the canyon mouth now, filling it with light.

Murphy cleared his throat. "Pour piss out of a boot?"

Midge laughed, almost choking on coffee. "I knew you'd like that—it was the first thing that came to mind. But I was right, Al, and you know it."

"You know," he said, looking out across the park, listening to the birds, the steam coming off the grass.

"Nobody else has ever called me Al. Not once. Not even my mother."

"I was right, Al," she repeated.

"Yes. Yes you were. Dead right. Even if we do it wrong, it's better than the way we were."

"And that's the beauty of it," she said, leaning over to kiss him on the neck. "Nothing can go wrong . . ."

CHAPTER 6

THE work was staggering, unbelievable, and at one point—everything considered—when he was trying to use the mules to skid base logs for the cabin, he thought that if he had known how hard it was he might not have done it. Although he said nothing to Midge about it.

That first night they had made a list, or tried to make a list, of things to do and the order to do them in.

First had to be the stock. They needed a corral and feed bunks and a gathering pen. There were plenty of pine trees along the side of the valley to use for posts and rails. And Murphy had remembered saws, hammers, axes, and draw knives to peel the bark off but had forgotten—and he hoped to God it was the only major item he'd forgotten—to get a post hole digger.

So each post for the corral and gathering pen had to be hand-dug with a shovel, which meant that each hole had to be dug out much larger than necessary, the post put in, then the hole refilled and tamped to keep it stout. It was slow, hard work, and by the time they had the corral and pen done—new posts and rails shining like yellow honey in the sun—Murphy didn't dare think about building the cabin. He would just do it, do it without thinking.

The bell mare had been tied for the three days it took to make the corral—another six on the holding pen—and she rolled forever when he turned her into the enclosure. He'd been afraid to let her run because she was the only riding horse he had caught up. About half of the herd was broken, but he'd need one horse to catch more, and if they got away from him and he went after them on foot he might be a week walking—and then be lucky to catch them. He'd heard a story once of a man who spent close to a month trying to catch "tame" horses on foot. They kept just out of his reach, and the only way he'd finally caught them was to take a rifle and crease one of them across the top of his head. Rifles and men being what they were, Murphy thought, God only knew how many horses the man had killed before he managed to "crease" one.

With the corral done, Murphy had thrown a saddle over the mare. She popped a few times, but considering she hadn't been ridden for close on a month, she was surprisingly considerate and settled in just a few moments.

Getting another horse was a whole new problem. He and Midge wanted to take a day and see the rest of the valley, and Murphy had set his eye on a large brown gelding the horse broker had said was "well-broke to ride." He'd give Midge the mare, which Midge had named Porky, "because it's so round."

Murphy decided if the gelding was well-broke he had never seen a horse. The animal ducked the rope like a magpie. Not that Murphy was much with a rope—it was all he could do to throw it without strangling himself— but the gelding had the eye of an eagle, and when he saw the loop coming he'd just lay his ears and head down and let it slide over.

Of course, it didn't help that Midge was about doubled over with laughter watching them. Murphy rode the mare around the herd, letting her walk after the gelding until she was so close to him that Murphy could almost touch him; then Murphy would "throw" (almost drop) the loop at him, and the gelding would duck and he'd have to start over. Midge stood by the wagon, and before it was finished she was hanging on the side of the wagon, tears streaming down her cheeks as she laughed.

"You look like you're trying to drop a hankie on him," she yelled once. "You put the rope out so dainty and light. Like a lady dropping a hankie." And the gelding ducked again and Midge was off into another peal of laughter.

Finally Murphy got the rope on the gelding—which he had named about fourteen different names, none of which he could say in public—but if he thought the battle was over he was almost completely wrong. Oh, the gelding came to the rope easily enough—trotted right into the corral alongside the mare.

But when Murphy took his saddle off the mare to put on the gelding—he had the lighter, smaller saddle for Midge—the gelding laid his ears back and rolled his eyes.

"Does he do that because he's mad at you?" Midge asked. She was sitting on the top rail of the corral. In Casper she'd bought some small bib overalls and was wearing them, along with a denim workshirt—"just for working around the place," she'd said.

"No," Murphy answered, acid in his voice as he snubbed the gelding tighter to one of the corral posts, "it's because he's well-broke—like the man said." I'd sooner saddle a rattlesnake and ride it, he thought, watching the gelding's hooves. The problem, he thought, was that he was setting out to raise horses, and the truth was he couldn't ride very well. Oh, he knew some about them—what with cleaning stables in the army and riding horses all his life; he knew as much about them as most people. But most people didn't set out to raise horses. They just bought them and rode them. And that's all he'd done. They were just something to use.

Well, you jugheaded son of a bitch, he thought—when on the seventh try he finally got the saddle on the gelding's back and cinched down—I guess this is where I learn a little bit more about horses. Time to go to school. And he swung a leg over and pulled himself up.

The gelding blew up so fast Murphy didn't get his foot in the stirrup and he was back on the ground—upside down and tasting the corral dirt.

He tried again, and again he hit the ground before he was in the saddle.

"Hold his head down until I get set," he told Midge. He wrapped a short rope from the gelding's halter to the corral post and handed the end to Midge. "When I get up and in place unwrap the rope and turn him loose."

Midge nodded. "If you're sure that's what you want . . ."

And in truth he wasn't sure that's what he wanted, but it had to be done. The gelding held until he was in the saddle, until his feet were in the stirrups and he had settled his thighs into the saddle fork, until he was to the point of relaxing.

"Maybe he's done," he said quietly. "Maybe that's all . . ."

The gelding went insane. It left the ground with a leap that curved high as he arched his back and came down straight and stiff-legged, so hard that Murphy heard his teeth slam together. Before Murphy could catch his breath or figure out what to do next, the gelding spun and did another series—either two or fifty or a thousand, he couldn't count—of bucks that all came down stiff-legged and jolted Murphy so hard he thought his head was going to come out his hind end.

He grabbed the horn and hung on, determined to settle it; and when, at last, at long grinding last, the gelding stopped and stood, quivering and sweating, Murphy felt like every square inch of his body had been pounded into jelly.

"Well," Midge said, still sitting on the corral fence, "twenty-nine to go."

Strangely, once the edge was off the gelding, he settled in and proved to be reliable and steady. He let Murphy walk him around the corral, bring him up to a trot and easy canter, then back down—he felt as if he'd been mellow all his life.

A horse trainer in the army had told Murphy that the worse horses were when they bucked, the better they'd be when they settled down, but he had trouble believing the gelding wasn't going to get a second breath and kill him. He lifted his leg over and stood on the ground gingerly—both in pain and caution—and used his sleeve to wipe the blood from his nose and upper lip, but the gelding held and remained tame while they saddled Porky for Midge and rode up the center of the canyon, the grass rubbing the horses' bellies.

"He's a good-looking horse," Midge said, riding out to the side and looking at him. "Suits you. Big and easy moving. Just like you."

"I don't feel too easy moving right now," Murphy said, standing on the stirrups to lift his groin off the saddle. "I feel like somebody's been beating my behind with a fence post. . . ."

But Midge was gone, cantering out ahead. She was a good rider, in many ways better than Murphy. She sat the horse well, flowed with it when it ran, and Murphy made a mental note to ask her where she'd learned to ride. It struck him then that he knew almost nothing about her, and he wondered how that could be. They'd known each other for going on eight years, had been close for seven and a half. He knew her and was with her six months after she came to Cincherville with her husband, who was killed soon after their arrival. Yet Murphy knew nothing about her past. They talked and were close, but always when they had talked they spoke of the future—what they would be and do when they got away from Cincherville—never of the past.

Watching her ride, he wanted to know everything about her. She was wearing a man's hat made of felt, but the movement of the horse had loosened her hair and it flowed behind her like a veil. He wanted to know what she'd been like as a girl, what all her life had been like—her parents, brothers and sisters, childhood— everything. He knew she was from a farm in Iowa, that her father had wide shoulders (she'd compared them once to Murphy's, which were wide but curved, like a bear's) and that her mother had forgotten more about cooking than Midge knew (which Murphy doubted, having eaten her cooking for years). But that was it. Every other comment after that was looking forward, never back.

That was Cincherville, he thought, watching her suddenly wheel the little mare and wave at him to hurry. That town made everybody look ahead—trying to find a way out.

"Hurry, Al, you've got to see this!" she called, and Murphy nudged the gelding, half expecting to get thrown again. Surprisingly, the brown horse rolled into a gentle lope that ate the distance to Midge in a few moments.

"Isn't it beautiful?" she said, sweeping her arm ahead at a portion of the canyon they hadn't been able to see yet. "Isn't it just the most beautiful thing you've ever seen?"

Murphy let the gelding stop next to her and took his hat off, holding it to shield the light out of his eyes. The valley rose ahead of them in a shallow grade for two or three miles, angling off to the right—the north. It was all open and green, rich green, with grass from the mountains down to their feet. Except where the stream wound through the middle. Here aspens had grown, aspens and later cottonwoods, and where there were aspens there were beaver.

All down through the canyon the beaver had dammed the stream, making one pond that flowed in a short stream to the next for pond after pond, like a string of jewels. For over a mile the ponds fed into one another, and Murphy could see it all now. See what their lives would be.

They would raise horses in this private canyon, raise them and each year sell some to the army for remounts, and that's all they would hope for, want for—to live in this place and raise horses and get up in the morning and see the grass and be together. It all rolled into one picture for him and he wanted to tell her of it, but the words wouldn't come right. Instead he leaned over and down from the gelding and kissed her and saw that she knew he meant more. Meant all of everything there was to mean.

She knew.

CHAPTER 7

SOMEHOW it worked. Even though Murphy knew nearly nothing about how to farm, how to build a home or farm, somehow it worked. Day went into another day, week into another week, and a lean-to was made for the stock, and a rough cabin was up with split cottonwood shingles for a roof that almost didn't leak. Murphy put one window in it, which he covered with greased paper so it would let in at least some light (and he wondered where he had learned that when he did it) and he made a crude door with split green cottonwood logs. And at night when he fell into the bunk they had against the wall of the cabin, he had never been so tired—and never been so happy.

They made a want list. They needed a small kitchen stove—which would also heat the cabin—and a post hole digger (Murphy wrote that on the list in all capital letters), a small anvil, and food for the winter—flour and bacon and a hundred pounds of beans, and some of those new canned tomatoes and seeds for a garden.

Midge had brought some seeds, folded and wrapped in small paper packets the way they came from the seed catalogs, with pictures of the mature vegetables on the side. Murphy had shovel-dug a kitchen garden; and inside of a week the radishes were up, and the line of green small plants stopped him cold one morning as he walked to the corral to harness the mules and skid logs in.

Midge came out, holding a cup of coffee, and saw him stopped, staring down at the radishes, the harnesses draped over his shoulders.

"What's the matter?"

"I just realized I've never grown anything, never had anything but that goddam busted town and a gun and a nest of a bed in a cheap hotel. I've never . . . you know . . . grown anything—made anything live. That's it. I've been all these years on the hard side of it, stopping things, sometimes killing them, and I've never once planted a garden, made anything grow."

She said nothing, waiting, watching him quietly.

"There's a whole damn world out there that's been there all the time and I didn't know anything about it. People growing gardens and farming and just living, and all I saw was the back side of it. What a waste. What a goddam waste."

"No." She shook her head. "It's not a waste because you've got it now. Sometimes we have to do things we don't want to do for a while so we can do things we want later. It's some kind of rule."

"Some rule," he said, shrugging the harness higher onto his shoudler and turning once more for the corral. "Some goddam rule."

In early August they had their first fight.

The mornings were snapping cool, almost too cool, and there was a smell of coming fall in the air, though the days were hot and dry and flat. They had to make a supply run to Casper and fill their want list, get ready for fall—it could snow enough to stop them in September and then they'd be caught until spring—and at the last minute Midge decided to stay.

It was the rabbits that caused it. Later Murphy chewed on the question and tried to figure the one thing that made her stay. He decided it was the rabbits, because they came to the garden in the early morning out of the aspens up the side of the mountain. Cottontail rabbits as cute as pictures in a child's book. But they hit the garden like wolves, a bite here and there, and if they weren't chased out of the patch they'd ruin the whole garden. They shot a few and made stew of them, but they still came at night and Midge brooked no interference with her garden.

"We need those vegetables," she said. "And if I go with you, there won't be anything left when we get back."

"I'm not leaving you alone here," Murphy said stubbornly.

"And I'm not leaving the garden and everything else. There's the horses to watch and Porky to feed . . ."

"We'll turn her in with the herd, or take her with us."

"And the cabin. What if a bear turns up? You cut those bear tracks the other day on the north edge, remember? If a bear hits the cabin, he'll tear it apart."

"And you're going to stop him, I suppose."

"I'll have the rifle. Did you think you were the only person in the world who can shoot?"

And they'd gone back and forth that way until Murphy finally had to admit she was right. Somebody should stay with the cabin. It just made good sense. His real worry was the long riders—he couldn't get them out of his mind—but that had been more than two months ago. Nobody, not a single person, had come to the canyon, not Indian or white. So in the end, Murphy gave in. But he insisted on being certain she knew how to shoot, so he took her up the canyon to a place where the stream made a gravel bank and shoved some sticks in the sand and gave her the rifle.

"With a bear from the side, you aim across low through the shoulders and shoot more than once. Aim each shot carefully, but shoot more than once because they die slow. Really slow, and they can do a lot of damage even after they've been hit solidly. From the front aim at the center of the chest. Don't try to hit them in the head because the skull slants back and the bullet might glance off."

She held the gun. The stock had been chewed by a porcupine near the handgrip when Murphy had left the gun leaning against the cabin wall for a night and forgot it was there. Her hand looked small where it went through the lever. It was red and hard and tough-looking from working, but still it looked small and not suited to the steel hard edges of the lever, the dark curve of blued steel. The rifle was chambered for .45-70, still used the old blackpowder charges, made a mountain of smoke when it roared—and it roared like a thunderstorm with each shot—and had a recoil like getting hit in the shoulder and cheek with a hammer.

On the first shot, he showed her how to make a sight picture, how to hold at the base of what she was trying to hit—one of the sticks—how to lean into the recoil so her whole body would help absorb the shock, and how to squeeze the trigger. And still the kick of the rifle bruised her shoulder and left a small red spot on her cheek where her thumb hit. The bullet tore one of the sticks in half.

"That hurts," she said, rubbing her cheek.

"Nothing's free. You need a big bullet to get the job done, but it takes a lot of push to get a big slug working." Murphy levered another shell into the rifle. "And all that push comes back against your shoulder. Hold it tight and lean into it—here, do it again." He handed her the gun.

She raised it, barely got it into position, and scared of the coming recoil, closed her eyes and jerked the trigger. The barrel swung with the jerk and she shot a foot to the right.

"No, no. Always squeeze. When you pull like that you swing the barrel sideways. You want it to be a surprise every time the gun goes off. Squeeze slowly or the bullet won't get where you want it to go and you might as well not shoot. Now," he tucked the gun back into her shoulder, pulling her head down to the stock, "aim and squeeze, squeeze it again."

This time she was ready for it, and the big slug hit another stick. The recoil didn't set her back as much, and by the time she'd shot a half dozen more rounds Murphy admitted she could do all right.

"All right, with a bear you shoot like I said—across the shoulders. With a man you aim for the middle of the biggest part . . ."

"There won't be any trouble."

"I know, I know. But just so you know how to use it. A gun might hang on the wall or your hip for a year, two years, and not be necessary. But when you need it, if you need it, you'll need it fast and you'll need it right. So pay attention. With a man if you hit any part it will usually stop him, but you want to work the lever right away after the shot and get another round chambered and ready to use if you need it . . ."

He made her shoot more, another ten rounds, until the bank was torn to pieces by the impact of the bullets and she could work the lever and handle the rifle with at least some familiarity, although she still flinched a bit with the recoil.

Then they rode back to the cabin and he got the wagon ready to go. It was late afternoon and she was surprised when he started to harness the mules.

"Aren't you going to wait until morning?"

"It's been hot during the days and the mules work best when it's cool. I thought I'd run them all night and morning, then rest them through the hot part of the afternoon. They're in good shape, tough as cobs—I figure I can make it in three days each way."

It was, finally, time to leave and he hung back. The mules stomped and kicked—they weren't fond of starting work this late in the day—and he'd have to drive them hard for a few hours to get them settled into the collars. But still he held back.

"I'll be all right," she repeated, reading his thoughts, looking up at him as he sat on the wagon seat. "You go now . . ."

"You keep Porky ready in the corral. Keep the saddle handy."

"Just go. I'll be fine. Really."

At length he nodded and slapped the mules on their rumps with the loose end of the reins, cracked them twice before they started to move. Just before he entered the aspens by the stream to cross and head down the creek and out of the canyon he turned back.

Midge was standing there, one arm waving over her head, the other down at her side. Just as he looked a gust of wind blew her hair across her face, and she used her left hand to brush it back and hold it. She kept waving with her right and he waved back and kept waving until he was out of sight in the trees.

Silly, he thought—like a lovesick calf. Keep waving like that and staring back. He'd be gone six days, five if he whipped the mules a bit and the trail stayed dry. She'd be fine. Silly to look back that way.

But he tried to remember exactly how she looked when the wind took her hair, exactly everything about her and the way she was standing and waving, the sun on her face as she squinted and waved and smiled— every single little thing as he drove the mules out of the canyon toward Casper—and he didn't know why he pushed his memory that way, drove his memory to remember Midge as he drove the mules.

It was as if he thought the memory would be the same as having Midge with him.

CHAPTER 8

IT started raining as he pulled the wagon into Casper early on the third morning. He had made good time because it had remained dry and cool at night, and the mules had worked well. He had seen nobody and driven alone, except one night when he thought he saw a flickering campfire to the west, closer to the mountains; but he didn't want to take the time to investigate it and had lost sight of it almost at once. In ten minutes he had convinced himself that it was all in his mind, that there hadn't been a fire at all but that he'd been looking at a star low on the horizon.

It was only a light sprinkle—the clouds were not thick and they were moving fast and clearly it would be over soon—but the streets were instantly turned to mud. It hit him that he had never seen Casper dry or without mud. The mud was not the depth it had been before, but it was slick and the mules pulled sideways now and again as they made their way to the livery. There were not the crowds of people there had been before, but it was still early in the day. The same gnome of a man was there and he remembered Murphy and helped tie the mules in two stalls at the end of the stable. They used a couple of feed sacks to rub the mules down and get the rain off them.

"Grain them pretty heavy," Murphy said. "I worked them hard getting here and I'll be leaving tonight."

"I'll clean and trim their feet, too," the small man

said. "Extra dime per mule for that but they'll work better for you if their frogs are picked out clean and the edges burred off."

Murphy nodded and stopped near the door, looking out at the rain—it was already starting to clear off—and gathering his thoughts on what to do. First he'd go to the dry goods store and get all the material on the list, then to the land office to stake his claim to the canyon, then he'd get the hell out of town.

No, first he should say hello to Hiram. "Marshall around?"

The livery man paused. He had been cutting a chew of tobacco and he stopped with the knife halfway through the plug. "Why, no, we buried him better than three and a half weeks ago. Close on a month. Nice funeral too, not too dusty and just about everybody came. Hiram was a crude man, sometimes profane and loud to boot, but he got the job done and everybody liked him."

"What happened?"

"Why, they shot him, that's what happened. He was eating a big plate of sowbelly and spuds with brown gravy over to Mackson's café and some men rode up the hitch rail and shot him right through the front window. Didn't say hello nor boo nor nothing. Just pulled out rifles and set to putting about twenty holes in Hiram. He was sitting looking right out the window, too, like he always did, but it didn't help. They were shooting before he could set his fork down . . ."

"Men—how many men?"

Now he finished cutting the plug and put it in his mouth. "Nobody's sure about that. I seen 'em come by and thought they was six, but some said seven. One man swore it was eight. I know they put a powerful lot of lead through that window at Mackson's. It was a stump miracle that nobody else was hit though they say the cook—that would be Mackson's wife—wet herself when the bullets started coming through the kitchen wall, which lines up dead on the window, and that she still stutters some from it."

The long riders, Murphy thought—Teason and his men come back. Hiram—big, fat, solid. Bullets hitting him. Murphy thought instantly, intensely, of Midge.

He had to get back.

No, wait. Hiram's murder happened almost a month ago. Be reasonable now, he thought. Easy down, easy down. "Did anybody see them leave?"

"Who?"

"The riders. After they shot Hiram, did anybody see which way they rode out of town?"

"Not me. I heard the shooting, but I was in back of the barn and it was over when I got out to the street. It happened fast. Real fast. You might want to talk to the kid Hiram hired to be the jail swamper. Kid named Opher. He'd be over to the office, cleaning up. That's all he was good for, and now they up and made him deputy."

Murphy was walking before the man had finished speaking. The marshall's office—also the jail building— was across the street and down two doors, and he crossed the street in five hurried strides.

Either Murphy was getting old, really old, or Opher was little more than a child. He couldn't have started shaving yet. Red-blond hair and washed blue eyes, his hair slicked down with some kind of grease, a scrawny boy turned when Murphy opened the door and stepped inside out of the rain. He was wearing a Colt's in a hand-stitched raw leather holster tied to his leg, and the leg was so thin the gun wobbled when he turned. On his tow linen shirt he wore the same badge that had been on Hiram's chest.

"My name's Murphy, I used to know Hiram." Murphy held out his hand, but it seemed that he was playing games with a child who was pretending to be grownup. His hand dwarfed that of the boy and he felt baby fat.

"I know who you are," the boy said, his voice squeaking. "Hiram spoke about you. You were the law down in Cincherville. He said you was tougher than boiled owlshit. Is that right—are you that tough?"

God, Murphy thought, his nuts haven't dropped yet. His voice hasn't changed. He ignored the question. "I need to know more about the men who killed Hiram."

The boy shrugged. "Not much to know. Six or eight men rode up to Mackson's and shot him full of holes, then rode away. I tried to get people to go after 'em, but ain't nobody in this town with enough sand to fill a sock and I sure as hell couldn't go after 'em alone. So there you are."

"Which way did they leave?"

The boy thought for a moment. "Let's see, I was over at Tucker's dry goods sweeping out—I sweep out there once a day—and I looked out when I heard the shots and they went by south. Yeah, they rode out south. Why does that matter?"

Again Murphy ignored the question. If they went south they might be heading on down to Denver, or anywhere in between, but at least they weren't heading up the range, toward his canyon. Maybe. But they might have been figuring on being chased and gone south to throw any pursuers off, then turned and gone any direction. He thought immediately of the fire he'd either seen or thought he'd seen on the way down. And

Midge again, Midge in the canyon. He'd have to hurry, get back as soon as possible. He felt a deep, instinctive urgency. To hell with the claim and resting the mules. He'd get some goods at the store and head out. He turned to leave.

"Mr. Murphy," the boy stopped him. "Hiram set a lot of store by you. I thought maybe you could help me. Give me some advice on what to do now that I'm the law."

Murphy stopped and studied him. The boy was skinny, the gun belt wrapped time and a half around him, the iron flopping at his side, the silly badge hanging on his shirt, and Murphy could see it had him—the great lust had the kid. The lust that brought men to guns and violence and death again and again. It was in his voice, his manner, his shoulders, the way he tried to thicken his neck. The same lust that had the long riders and that once held Murphy so tightly, the stinking great lust that clamped young men in its legs and wouldn't let go until somebody, something, all things died. Jesus, Murphy thought, remembering his youth—was I like this, really like this? And he knew that he was, that he had been exactly the same, and that after he was dead and this boy was dead some new young boy would get the same lust.

"Kid," he said, sighing, "the best advice I can think to give you is to take that goddam gun off your hip and throw it and the badge in the outhouse and walk away— but you won't do that, will you?"

The boy shook his head. "I can't."

The pride, Murphy thought—the goddam pride was on him. All gun and dumb. The law. "Then there's nothing I can say to help you. Nothing." He wheeled and went back into the street, driven now to get away from Casper, to get back to the canyon.

He stopped at the bank long enough to change his paper money to gold coin, which was easier to spend, and he almost trotted to the store with his list.

"Fill it the best you can," Murphy told the storekeeper. "I'll be back with a wagon in twenty minutes..."

And he was out the door of the store and across to the livery. August heat was up now, though it was still early in the day, and the mules had settled into the cool shade of the livery to rest, dozing and whipping flies with their tails. There was nearly a war when Murphy threw the collars around their necks and started to harness them.

The jenny took a cut at him with her teeth that was fast as a rattler, and when he jumped back the jack kicked sideways and came close to pushing his bellybutton through his backbone. "Ear him," Murphy told the livery man. "Ear him so I can get the harness on him . . ."

"They ain't going to want to pull a whole hell of a lot." The little man spit and took a mouthful of the jack's ear and bit down hard. The mule quivered and stood still, looking at the ground while Murphy finished buckling the collar, wrapped the hames around it, and strung the supports and traces back over the animal's rump. The jenny was still short but she didn't kick, and he harnessed her after only two halfhearted biting attempts.

"They was just getting into standing," the livery man said. "And I didn't get their hooves picked for you. You might get a mile out of town and they'll stop on you and there ain't nothing you can do if that happens. A mule won't run to the whip."

Murphy finished harnessing in silence, working fast now. He manhandled the wagon out of the open center of the livery into the street and brought the mules out one at a time to hook them into the tongue and single-trees. The livery man kept up a running commentary on mules the entire time.

When Murphy was finished he gave the man a dollar—though he hadn't left the mules overnight and they hadn't been grained—and climbed into the wagon seat to move them over to the store to load the goods Tucker was stacking on the boardwalk on the edge of the street. The rain had let off but the storekeeper had found a tarp and covered the perishables anyway.

There was an instant mutiny. The jenny simply stood when he clucked at them and popped the reins on their rumps. But the jack actually pulled backwards and half sat down, every muscle in his body rebelling.

The livery man went forward and grabbed their halters, swearing, while Murphy loosened the end of the reins and took a mighty cut through the air with the loose end. Dust fairly flew off the jack's hind end, and he lurched forward almost against his will. As soon as he moved the jenny followed him also involuntarily, but Murphy popped them again at once and the livery owner jerked the halters and they kept moving.

In three or four steps they were over the rebellion. Murphy nodded his thanks and moved them up the street a hundred yards to shake them out, then brought them around to the store.

"I don't have some of the things," Tucker said, helping him load. "But what I had is here."

Murphy worked with quiet urgency, packing goods.

When everything was loaded the wagon was full to a level even with the bed. "Some material," he added at the last. "Give me some pieces of material. For a dress."

"How much?"

"I don't know. Some. Some pretty material—enough for two dresses."

Tucker moved back in the store and came out with material wrapped in butcher paper. "I put in a little calico and three yards of flowered light cotton . . . she'll like that for a summer dress."

Murphy paid with double eagles, took some change in paper—not bothering to count it but jamming the money in his pocket—and was out the door and in the wagon seat before the storekeeper had closed the till. The mules didn't hesitate, hitting the collars immediately, lunging to get the heavier wagon moving; but still he snapped the reins on them a couple of times. It was the wrong thing to do—"Whip a horse early, get in late," was an old cavalry adage—but he couldn't help himself.

All he could think of was Midge and that stupid damn fire. His mind had changed now, flopped like a fish dying on the bank of a river, and in his thoughts the fire was no longer something from his imagination but real. No longer a star against the mountain sky but actual flames where somebody had stopped for the night.

And it must have been a large fire to show so far away, a big bonfire.

And the only reason to have a large fire was to warm a large group of men.

The long riders.

And Midge.

And that was all he could see or think as he whipped the mules out of Casper.

CHAPTER 9

HE paid for working the mules early.

Even pulling the heavier load he didn't let up on them. Part of him said to ease off, that driving the mules that hard was insane and that he was wrong to worry. There was no logic in thinking Midge was in danger, no reason to it. If he thought sensibly about it he could see that, and that he should have let the mules rest, that she was probably all right.

But there was a feeling, a hunch, a drive he couldn't explain. Seeing the fire or star or whatever it was had left a germ of worry, and when he'd heard that the riders shot Hiram it fueled the worry, and now he couldn't stop, couldn't think sensibly. Too many times he had followed hunches, times when it meant the difference between his life or death, and found them to be true; and now he could not deny the feeling, could not stop acting on it any more than if he were still the law in Cincherville.

Speed was everything to him but he paid, and paid dearly, for working the mules early and not pacing them out. Toward evening of the second day the jack went down. He had always heard that a mule had more sense than a horse and would quit pulling before he hurt himself, where a horse would pull himself to death, but the jack pulled himself right into the ground.

Just before dark the jack snorted some blood from his nostrils and blew and went down. Murphy jumped

67

from the seat, swearing at himself for being so stupid, and unhooked the trace chains on both mules. He manhandled the jack back up, unhooked the harness and removed it, speaking low to the mule while he worked. Had he not been so worried he would have been more grateful and would have wondered why the jack had given so much. Mules just didn't do that, or at least that's what everybody said, all about how a mule would quit on you.

When Murphy took the collar off his neck, the jack leaned against him like a drunk, and Murphy led him gently off to the side. He would come around in time—two, three days without work and eating grass and some grain—but Murphy didn't have time to stay with him. He'd just have to let him fend for himself and come on to the canyon when he felt like traveling.

He unharnessed the jenny and took her collar off as well. She was smaller but much tougher than the jack—the females tended to carry their weight better than the larger males, didn't tire as much, and seemed to have more heart as well. He was still eight or ten hours from the canyon, and that was riding. Walking in high-heeled boots might take fifteen hours.

Unless he could ride the jenny, he thought, studying her in the twilight. She was settled enough. It might work. He used his pocket knife to cut the reins and make them short enough to ride on her back instead of in the wagon. Then he gave her a handful of oats—the jack actually turned the oats down—and debated resting her before leaving. If he stayed an hour and rested the jenny she might move faster for longer, but she also might just kick his tail up around his neck when he got on her.

He decided to ride her tired and see if she would

stand for it, and to his surprise when he swung a leg over she acted as if she'd been ridden all her life. There was a little sag as she tightened her back to take his weight, but she straightened at once and held him easily.

He gave her some heels and she set off at a trot that jarred his teeth loose—no pace and all jump—but she didn't buck, and he eased his weight up on her shoulders to get the bounce out of his groin and took it.

She was tired. He couldn't push her but he rode her half an hour, then walked ten minutes, then rode another half hour and kept alternating that way through the night. Whenever they crossed a stream he got off and let her drink and eased her for five or six minutes, but never long enough for her to stiffen and start resting.

Toward dawn she finally stopped trotting and wouldn't pick the pace up even when he heeled her. She kept walking, but that was it and he had to take it. Exhaustion was like a heavy weight on his own back as well, and he fought to keep his eyes open. He was going on four days without any sleep and twice caught himself hallucinating. Out ahead once he saw a man on a horse beckoning and waving to him, and Murphy drew his Smith but when he aimed it was all gone, all in his mind. The grass was empty ahead in the gray new light and the mule gave no sign of having seen anything. And again he saw a buffalo, a white buffalo, almost silver, standing side-on as he rode by, and it frightened him without his knowing really why. But when he tried to turn and see it better as he passed, it disappeared. All tired pictures, sleep pictures.

When the light was full to his right he looked ahead and left and saw the twin buttes standing about six miles away. It was cloudy, but the kind of cloud that didn't bring rain. With the clouds the light had a flat quality, so the buttes seemed to be cut out of thick, flat paper, seemed to be something from a set—like the backdrop of a traveling theater-show that had once come to Cincherville.

The jenny knew where she was as well and gained some strength from it, and her walk seemed stronger. He jumped off her and led her to give her a break, and was trudging that way, holding the reins, his head down and half asleep—thinking he was absolutely crazy to be doing this for nothing more solid than a flickering light that might have been a fire, thinking he would joke with Midge about it and how cross she would be that he had hurried and left the wagon standing, thinking they could come back for it later and how they would laugh at his silliness, thinking all these tired thoughts in his tired mind—when he saw the tracks.

In front of him, covering the ground, were the tracks of many horses, all heading out of the canyon. He was not very good at reading tracks, had only had to track men or horses a few times in his life, but he knew there were many—the belt of tracks was close to twenty yards across and the prints were thick over one another.

And of course, he thought, that could be the horse herd. His herd. Murphy's herd. That would be the horse herd leaving the canyon. For a second, perhaps two long seconds, he allowed the hope to live that they were merely wandering. The stud had taken them out of the canyon looking for better grass. Midge probably was involved with the garden or they had come out at night when she was asleep and she didn't see them leave . . . but hell, that didn't work either. If they were wandering they wouldn't stay in such a tight group.

The fear in him turned to a core of heat, a white hot

terror that made his breath come in jerks. Close on that way, packed horse on horse as the tracks were, meant the animals were being driven. They weren't wandering or foraging but being pushed, kept in a tight herd and pushed hard. He fought an impulse to jump on the jenny and whip her into the ground. It was still better than five miles to the buttes and she could do little more than walk.

He studied the ground and each print more carefully, and in ten paces he saw the first imprint of a shod hoof, which clinched it—the horses were being driven by men. His stomach turned and for a moment he thought he was going to vomit. There had been a hidden hope, a wish against reality that the horses were somehow wandering in a tight group. Now that was gone. He had never felt such fear, fear not for himself but fear for another—it was like a knife twisting in him. Panic came, numbing panic, and for long moments he stopped walking and simply stood, staring down at the tracks, trying to think, trying to make his mind work.

Then the old patterns took over. These were men. He knew men, he had worked against the wrong kinds of men all his life. He knew this, knew of this, knew what to do. This was what he did. This, he thought, is all I'm good for—just this.

First he had to find Midge, make sure she was all right, then handle the men, get the horses back. It was that simple. First Midge.

The tracks of the herd swung away to the north—had they come south he would have run into them—and he hesitated momentarily. If they had taken Midge, he would be wasting valuable time going up into the canyon. He should set out on the tracks at once. But if Midge had gotten away from them, she might be hiding in the canyon—he could not bring himself to think of anything worse—or she might need help. Besides, the jenny was in no shape to start a trip, nor for that matter was he; both of them needed rest, grain for the jenny, water, some hay, and a saddle if they had left one. He needed two hours of sleep, solid eyes-closed rest, before he began anything hard. He wasn't sure he could sleep, but he needed it. His body was running on thought alone.

He started trotting, still leading the jenny—not a long-legged run, not even fast, but more a shuffle, trying to balance on the heels of his boots as he trotted. In a quarter mile he was blowing, and he mounted the jenny for another quarter mile, letting her walk while he caught his breath, then he was down to trot for another quarter, then back up; and the buttes, the goddam buttes, wavered in his eyes and didn't seem to get any closer.

CHAPTER 10

THERE was a silence in the canyon that was almost thick as he followed the stream in through the aspens and cottonwoods. An unnatural silence. The birds seemed to have stopped their constant noise, and the water in the stream ran muted, pushing through his mind in a hushed roar.

Even from a quarter mile it was possible to see the cabin had been hit hard. The door hung on one leather hinge, pulled out and turned half over, and one corner was scarred and black where they had tried to fire it and the flames hadn't taken.

There was no smoke. His mind filed it automatically. No smoke, which meant it was long out. They had been gone a long time.

"Midge!"

His voice cracked—his throat was dry and felt brittle—and he moistened his lips and bellowed it again.

"Midge! I'm home—it's me!"

Nothing. Something skittered sideways from the cabin and he recognized it as a squirrel without thinking.

He dropped the reins on the jenny—she stopped immediately, didn't graze, just stopped—and ran the last fifty yards to the cabin.

They had tried at two corners to fire it—one at the front, the other at the rear—but both fires had gone out before the logs, which were still slightly green, could take the flames. The bottom leather hinge on the door had been cut and the door pulled out at the bottom.

Was she in there then? Oh God, was she in there while the bastards cut the hinge and pulled the door out, in there waiting, hearing them, the bastards the bastards the

bastards . . .

His heart, his soul, ached with dread as he went inside, but the cabin was empty and strangely not terribly disturbed. The table, a split-log rig he'd made one afternoon, was not even turned over, and a set of split shelves against one wall still held some flowered dishes Midge had brought that he hadn't known about until she unpacked them. He had teased her about bringing them, could not believe she'd brought them unbroken all that way in the wagon, and she was inordinately proud of them.

One thing on the floor—a woolen shawl she had worn on cool evenings—caught his eye and he picked it up, tried to feel her in it, smell her in it. He held the wool against his cheek. It had taken coolness from the earth floor but he could smell her lavender water. Even in the cabin, the primitive cabin, she had bathed with the gently scented water and it was in the wool, mixed with the earth.

Please God. He did not know what to ask further. Just that. Please God.

He went back to the front of the cabin. "Midge!"

It roared out and up the canyon walls, bounced back to him, and echoed back and forth. If she was in the canyon she had to hear it, had to know he was there.

Unless she was hurt. Down and hurt.

Perhaps unconscious.

He leaned against the cabin wall—his body was nearly

done, nearly done as the jack had been done, done and fallen—and he tried to think, tried to make his brain work right. Even his vision was starting to blur. If they had her, if they had taken her with the horses, he had to go after them, but he would have to rest first.

If they didn't have her, then where was she, what had happened?

If she had gotten away from them somehow, hidden from them, she would come. If she heard him. Perhaps his voice wasn't carrying enough.

He pulled the Smith and fired twice over his head. The sound, cutting the still silence, was deafening; and the jenny, still standing where he'd dropped her lines, jerked and moved three or four steps to the side.

And what the hell good would that do, he thought. If she heard the gun, what would it mean to her? Just that somebody was shooting a gun. It wouldn't make her come to him. Even if she could.

Please God.

All he could think to do was walk further up the canyon and look for tracks or some other sign. If he didn't move he was going to drop where he stood.

He started moving, one foot in front of the other—a dim form of reason taking him, thinking he would make one sweep and look for her and then rest and go after them if he didn't find her—the Smith still hanging in his hand. And he had not taken ten steps when he saw movement up the canyon.

It was a horse. At the distance—close on three-quarters of a mile—he could not tell what horse, but it was a dark horse. Small. And moving strangely. Not just head out to the side so it wouldn't step on its reins, but hopping. He shook his head, squinted to see better. There was no rider.

He looked to the jenny, thinking of riding to meet the horse, but she was done, and she stood as she'd stopped after he shot in the air, her head down, asleep.

He started trotting again, moving slowly toward the horse. He knew the motion but could not remember in his fog from where or what it meant. Somewhere in his memory a horse had done that, hopped that way—oh, yes. In the army. A horse with a broken front leg had hopped that way. Held one leg in the air and hopped until they shot it.

He stared at the horse as he tried to run. It would hop ten or twelve times, then stop, then hop and come to a halt again, and when he had covered a couple of hundred yards he could see the horse well enough to identify it.

It was Porky.

And still closer he could see that it was saddled and bridled, stepping now and again on the reins as it hobbled and skipped forward.

Finally he was at the horse and he could see the extent of the injury. The right front leg was broken, a compound fracture of the main upper leg bone, which struck out white in the sunlight. There was very little blood, which meant the leg had broken suddenly, in a fall—sudden breaks rarely bled—and the pain had driven the animal into shock. Its eyes were wide and it seemed not to recognize Murphy, tried to hop past him, driven by some urge to get back to the cabin, running on nerves alone.

Murphy shot her in back of the ear and resumed trotting. Midge must have ridden Porky—that's all he could think. Not to where or why Midge had ridden, just that she had. If the horse fell and Midge were hurt he had to get to her.

He shuffled without seeing the canyon, without seeing anything but the next step, his boots rolling to the
side now with his run because his ankles were tired and
weak, the gun still in his hand from when he'd shot the
mare; and in half a mile he looked ahead, near where
the stream entered the canyon from the mountains—
another half of a mile—and he saw crows. Eight or nine
of them wheeling up from the ground, then settling
back down. Crows. Crows that came to find the dead.
From miles away they could sense it, smell it, feel it.
Crows.

No, he thought. Not this time. This time you're
wrong. This time you've got to be wrong. Not this time.
Please God. Please God . . .

He found her in a small gully.

At first he went past her because the crows had risen
from slightly further up the creekbed, and when he
came to where the crows had been he had a moment of
hope because he found an old, dead buffalo calf—little
more than bones—and thought that was what had
drawn the crows.

But as he walked back down the gully he came around
a corner and found her and he wished that his eyes
hadn't worked, that his mind hadn't worked to see it.

She was lying face down in the sand at the side of the
gully wall, one shoulder bent partly under, her left arm
back with the hand and fingers up, her right arm out
ahead with the hand down and her face, her face,
canted sideways down into the dirt. She was wearing one
of his old workshirts and her bib overalls and small
button shoes—God, were her feet that small?—and most
of her hair was tied back with a scarlet ribbon.

No. It was an explosion in his brain. NO!

He ran to her side and fell to his knees, turned her

over, and pulled her up and held her. Some sand clung to her cheek and he brushed it away and more sand was in her right eye, which was partially open, and he tried to brush that away, and her hair had fallen into her face and he pushed that back away from her face—as she had always done herself—and he made her live in his mind, in his thoughts he made her live and smile and see him, and he kissed her on the mouth, the forehead, the eyes; made her come alive for all the screaming anguish in his heart but he could not.

Could not make it happen. There was not life there, not a single thing of life left. Her cheeks were cold and some puffiness had come in and her eyes were glazed and gone with a look he had seen many times on men who were dead but never, never like this, in this way.

Oh no oh no oh no . . . a chant, a moan as he held her and rocked back and forth, held her and tried to make it not be, tried to make death not be with all that he was, sat in the noonday sun and rocked with the small body in his arms and could think of nothing except that it couldn't be.

It couldn't be.

It couldn't be.

CHAPTER 11

FOG.

A strange haze over everything, over and in everything. He walked, breathed, lived, but did not know how, did not really know what was happening, only that certain things had to be done.

He carried Midge's body back to the cabin, staggering with it and the exhaustion—four days without sleep except a doze now and again on the wagon seat—and all the way he talked to her, told her of the things he'd bought in Casper, the material for the dresses, the food, the seeds for the garden, told her as if she were awake and listening. Her head rolled loosely and her body hung slack and there was the smell that goes with bodies, but he pretended not to notice it, not to know it, pretended to himself and walked with her and talked with her as he always had.

At the cabin he laid her gently on the bed inside and used some water from the stream and a damp rag to wash her face. There was still some sand in the corners of her eyes and nostrils and he cleaned these out as well. Then he took the shovel and went to the place above the cabin where she liked to sit and look at the valley and sip coffee.

"It's out of the bugs," she once said, speaking of the flies and gnats that stayed around the barn lean-to and corral, drawn to the horses. "There's a small breeze to keep the bugs away and you can see all the way to the end of the valley."

Murphy dug a grave there, just where she liked to sit. A part of him thought he should take her back to Casper to the graveyard and have a minister talk over her. Midge had firm beliefs about God, much more than Murphy—especially now, now that he viewed God as little more than an enemy—but his practical side knew it wasn't possible. It was hot, and two or three days, even if he found the jack and got both mules to somehow pull the wagon—if the wagon was still there— would be out of the question.

So he dug the grave. It took him all of that day. There were rocks to pick out and chew at with the shovel and he wanted it deep, six feet at least, to keep out any bears or coyotes; and when it was finally done he hacked a ledge in the side near where she would lay and brought all the things she loved except one. He brought the dishes and her favorite cup and some silverware she had saved from an aunt and a locket and a small wooden box with a pair of genuine pearl earrings and placed them gently, one by one, on the small ledge in the side of the grave.

All he held back of the things she loved was the shawl he'd found on the earth floor of the cabin. That he kept, tied loosely around his neck for the time being, but later wrapped carefully in a piece of butcher paper and carried inside his shirt; and at present he didn't know he'd done it, only that he needed some part of her with him.

When the grave was done and all her objects in place, he wrapped the body—no, he thought of it as her, wrapped her, wrapped Midge—in a blanket from the bed, wishing they'd had sheets because they seemed more refined, and placed her carefully, gently, in the cool earth at the bottom of the deep pit.

He lowered the blanket from her face and kissed her one more time, covered her face again, and climbed one last time from the grave and stood for several minutes at the edge, trying to think God-thoughts or remember any of the burying words; but nothing came but hate, raw hate for anything Godlike, hate for anything but the small body below him, and so he stopped. She would not have wanted hate.

He took the shovel and began to fill the grave, putting the earth on her head last—trying not to think of anything when he did that—and he kept at the filling with a steady pace into darkness and worked after dark until it was filled and the fresh earth was mounded and tamped. Then he brought the lamp from the cabin, unscrewed the wick, and poured the fuel oil in a thin stream around the grave. This, too, he learned in the army. In field graves which had to be dug shallow they carried fuel oil to dampen the earth and keep predators out. The smell drove them away.

At the last, working now in the moonlight that came white and flat just after dark because the moon was already up, he fashioned a crude cross from two pieces of wood taken from the table in the cabin and dug the monument into the end of the grave dirt, packing it tightly with stones.

When it was all done, all done and gone, he was done as well. When the cross was in place he could not move more, could not even get up, but kneeled in exhaustion, kneeled in a kind of prayer, kneeled in a kind of death at the head of the grave and closed his eyes, still kneeling, and became unconscious . . .

His eyes were open but he wasn't sure he was awake and didn't care in any case. It was still dark, he was still kneeling at the end of the grave. His legs were asleep and numb and his arms hung at his sides. He had drooled and he wiped his chin. Dust swirled around him, making him squint.

He raised his head. The night sky had turned while he slept, gone from clear moonlight to a wind and clouds whipping overhead. They seemed so low he felt in them, felt them going by on the sides. He had not been thinking, just reacting, doing, and he suddenly hated himself. It had to come, hating himself, and if anything he was surprised it had taken so long.

He hated himself first for bringing Midge to the valley, to this valley, then for leaving to go to Casper, for leaving her alone. He could see all the things that had happened, as they must have happened.

She must have seen them coming somehow. Maybe she'd been working in the garden, the silly little garden, when she'd seen the long riders coming up the valley, and she had run to the corral and saddled the mare to get away. They had seen her, of course. If she could see them they must have seen her and chased her.

The rifle. Did she take the rifle? Did she try to stop them with the rifle?

No matter. She must have just run, trying to reach the end of the canyon, trying to reach some kind of safety she thought was there; and the little mare tried to jump the gully and came down wrong, broke its leg, went over, and dumped Midge so that her neck was broken, and he hated himself for every part of all of it.

Hated himself for the saddle and the horse and the canyon and the mules and Casper and her run and her fall and her death—every single damn thing that happened made the hate more powerful as he thought of it and he knew then that he could not live. It wasn't just that he didn't want to live, but he could not live, could not be with the self-hate; and his hand pulled the Smith from the holster and his thumb eared the hammer back and he put the barrel in his mouth and in the swirling dust and wind and scudding clouds, kneeling at the end of the grave he began to squeeze the trigger. If he thought anything then, at that moment that was to be his last, if he thought anything it was that it was a proper end for him, blowing his damn brains out while he squatted in the dirt. His finger took up the slack on the trigger and he tried to think of Midge in the last second but he couldn't . . . could think of nothing but hate.

And it was hate that saved him,

How could it be that Midge could die and he would die but they would live? The question came in from the edges, slid in sideways. How could that be? How could it be that all Murphy loved could be dead and destroyed, ripped and killed and gone, and those bastards would live?

"*Ahhhhnnnnggg.*" It was part moan and part animal sound, almost a growl, and he did not know he made it.

It could not be. He lowered the Smith, let it hang in the dirt next to his leg. He could not live with it, live with the searing self-hate, but neither could they live— the long riders. Those who had come and destroyed everything had to be ended. He thought it that way. Not killed but ended.

They had to be ended.

He dropped the Smith back into the holster and tried to stand. His legs immediately collapsed and he fell on his side, fire roaring up and down both legs as the circulation started again. He reached down and massaged them, worked the muscles to get them going again, and tears came now for the first time. Not tears of loss, not tears of pity.

He cried in rage. It was a hot crying, a savage thing as he lay on his side rubbing his legs, hating the legs for not working, rubbing them and thinking all the while they must end.

They must end.

CHAPTER 12

HE did not have a plan. Everything hinged on the hate, and it made for no sensible thoughts or plans.

He moved, but without thinking. He would have to ride, he knew that, would have to ride to follow them, find them, and so he would need a saddle. His mind worked slowly ahead, plodded. He walked back to the dead mare—crows and now buzzards rose in a flock from the rapidly warming carcass—and took the saddle from her. The dead horse was heavy and he had to heave it over to get the cinch out, and when he rolled it the stink floated up and made him sick.

Vomiting made him thirsty, and he dragged-carried the saddle and bridle and blanket back to the cabin, then drank out of the stream where it came into the pond. He washed his face with water and felt more awake. He felt he should eat. He wasn't hungry, did not think he would ever feel hunger again, but knew that he should eat to regain some strength or he would not be able to function.

There was no food. They had stripped the cabin of everything edible, but he found radishes and onions in the garden. He brushed them off and ate them, tasting only wood, swallowed dryly, ate more, and drank again from the stream. There was food back at the wagon, some bacon and flour, if the wagon wasn't stripped bare, and some canned peaches and tomatoes.

He drank still more water and used it to fill his

stomach. It was nearly mid-morning now, and he felt like moving, getting on with it. The jenny was near the pond, eating in the short grass along the edge. She had been dried out as well as hungry, and between the water and grass she was looking much better. The muscle on her back, where mules stored both fat and water, had filled out, and she had spring to her step. An old sergeant had told him mules came back quicker than horses—they could be damn near dead and be packed the next day—and he believed it now. If he'd pushed horses as hard as he'd pushed the mules he'd have had to shoot them.

He tried to approach her but she shied away, stepping just ahead of him. He had no rope—they had taken a coil of line he had in the lean-to as well—but there was a double handful of oats left in the bottom of a bag, and he scooped them up and held them out. The jenny came for the oats and he let her eat out of one hand while he took her halter with the other.

He put the bridle on her first to keep control, then tied the reins off at the corral fence and saddled her with the blanket and saddle from the mare. The death stink was still in the blanket, and the jenny tried to reach around and pull it off, taking a halfhearted bite at his hand as well.

"No, dammit." He slapped her nose. She whipped her head around and rolled her eyes at the smell but didn't reach again. She drew breath and held it when he cinched her up, which meant she must have been saddled before—to know that, to know how to hold her breath while he tightened it and let it out to loosen the cinch when he finished. So she had been ridden before he got her, enough to learn the cinch trick. Maybe the jack had been ridden as well. If he found the jack and he could be brought back Murphy would have two mounts. He could alternate and ride twice as much.

He waited on her until she couldn't hold it any longer but blew out, then he pulled it tight before she could take another breath and tied it off.

The saddle was small, almost tiny. It was Midge's, and he let the stirrups out as much as they'd go, but they still looked too short.

He had no choice. They had taken his saddle as well— they must have packed one or two of the horses in the herd to take all the stuff they had; even the pitchfork and axe were gone. The only reason they'd missed the shovel was because Midge had put it beneath the door log in front, where it was handy to shoo rabbits out of the garden.

Midge. He thought suddenly, intensely, of her and for a second couldn't stand it, and he hung on the side of the mule until it passed. Thinking of the shovel and Midge chasing rabbits out of the garden with it, running in her nightdress, brought her back to him, and he started to wish-hope-believe again that she wasn't dead, but he knew she was, turned his mind upside down with it. He shook his head, wiped his eyes, swore under his breath, and turned back to the mule. There was only one thing to do, and to do it he had to ride the jenny.

He tied the left rein to his wrist. He couldn't take a chance on losing her if she threw him. He pulled on the horn twice hard to get her set, she braced for him, and he threw a leg over.

She didn't buck.

He couldn't believe it. When he had ridden her bareback she'd been so tired he figured she couldn't buck. But now, fresh, with water and grass and a mouthful of oats, he'd thought she'd tear him apart.

He gave her some heel and she moved forward, and had he not been so preoccupied, he would have thought on what a find she was; tough as a cob, willing to go and gentle to boot. She seemed to wait for his command, which was rare in a good horse and almost nonexistent in mules.

But his thoughts were elsewhere. It was necessary to ride to where Midge had fallen. The town lawman in him had taken over and he would have to read sign. They would have left some tracks there, as they had around the cabin, and he needed everything he could get. The tracks he had seen in and around the cabin were muddled, one over the other as they had stomped around, and he couldn't pin any of them down—they were just blurs and smudges. It might not help, but one of them might have a cut boot heel or other mark he could use later for identification.

He took the mule into a canter—her trot was vicious— and loped up the valley to the gully where Midge had fallen.

It pulled some out of him to look at it again and he held back at first. But again something outside of him took over, and he started to circle on foot, looking for marks or tracks or other signs. But he could see nothing except his own tracks and a solitary set of bootprints in the sand near where Midge's body had lain. There was a nick near the toe of the left foot—the kind of nick made when an axe skips off a piece of wood and hits the boot lightly—and the right heel seemed to be rounded under, almost as if the man walked in a rolling limp.

He had stood here; the son of a bitch had stood right here and looked down at her. He must have chased her here and when she fell, he got off his own horse and came forward, thinking he had her. But he saw she was dead and stood, staring down at her. The bastard. Stood right here. And he was alive and she was dead. The bastard.

Murphy felt it rising in him, the rage, and he shook his head. There had to be more than just one set. It made no sense. Had just one man in the group chased her? In his mind's eye he saw them all after her, harrying her, chasing her down like wolves, and he couldn't find another set of tracks. He made a large circle, a hundrd yards across, but saw nothing more. Just the scuff tracks of the mare trying to get back to the cabin on three legs.

So only one of them had come. Perhaps only one of them had seen her while the rest of them were busy in the cabin or something, had chased her alone because he wanted her for himself.

An almost insane anger exploded in him, thinking of the man chasing her, thinking of her running. He had to stop it. It grew in him so fast, so full of flame and hatred, that he couldn't control it, and the anger would keep him from getting anything done.

He had held the reins to the jenny all this time—he still didn't trust her completely—and she suddenly jerked at his hand and made a whickering sound, staring down the valley.

He saw something moving half a mile off, and his hand went immediately to the Smith at his belt; but almost at once he recognized the jack.

It was moving well enough—must have been eating and drinking all this time near the wagon and gotten strong enough to follow them in.

Murphy climbed back on the jenny and rode toward the other mule. He still had no way to rope him, but he knew the jack would follow the jenny so he rode on past and headed out of the valley.

When he was across from the cabin he stopped and looked up from the pond to the grave. Until then he had no idea of a plan, but it suddenly came over him and he nodded to the grave.

"I'll be back in a bit," he said. "I'll take care of this and I'll be back . . ." And he knew then that when it was done, if he still lived, he would come back here and end it with her as he'd started to do kneeling by the grave. There was, now, nothing in his life worth the living.

Just this job, he thought, heeling the jenny—just this job of hate and then there will be nothing. Everything and anything good that ever happened to me is in a hole in the ground . . .

CHAPTER 13

NOBODY had bothered the wagon. Two coyotes jumped from the box and skittered away when he rode up on the jenny. They had been into the flour and found a corner of the bacon, but most of the bacon was back under some feed sacks and they hadn't been able to get at it. He emptied the flour sack on the ground. He would have no use for flour and needed the empty bag. He also dumped most of the hundred-pound sack of oats, keeping about fifteen pounds in the bag. When he dumped the oats the jack came forward. He had followed them out of the canyon but kept his distance until now. The pile of oats on the ground was too much temptation for him, and when he leaned down to start eating Murphy caught his halter.

He used the thin rope from the wagon to tie him off, but let him eat for a bit first. Not enough to sicken him or founder him, but enough to make up for the last six days of rough work. Oats would go into mules or horses like fuel oil. He had seen horses in the army close to dead come back in two hours with oats or barley.

Murphy had tied the jenny to the other side of the wagon box, loosening the cinch to give her a rest. He took two pounds or so of oats around to her as well and let her eat while he sorted out what he had to take.

He would travel light. The riders would be going slow, with the herd, and if Murphy traveled light he shouldn't have any trouble catching them. Even in the four, maybe

91

five days since they'd left they couldn't have gone more than twenty miles a day, eighty or a hundred miles at the most. He could make forty, fifty miles a day on the jenny. So he'd catch them in two days, maybe three.

That's all the food he needed. That's all he could plan. Enough food to catch the bastards. He didn't think past that, and if he had thought further he probably wouldn't have changed his mind. Seven or eight heavily armed men, and all he had was the Smith and a box of shells. When he did catch them it wasn't likely he'd need food afterwards.

He'd take some bacon, some canned tomatoes and peaches, and on second thought he scooped up about five pounds of flour from the pile on the ground and wrapped it in a piece of paper tied off with a bit of leather thong. He'd have the bacon grease and he could make bannock bread—a trapper had shown him how to do it. Just flour and water for dough and fry it in grease. He didn't have any salt but the salt in the bacon grease would flavor it.

Midge, he thought—Midge would have snorted thinking of bannock bread. He'd never told her about bannock bread. Just about like eating wood dipped in axle grease, he thought—that's how he would have told her. Take a piece of pine and soak it in axle grease and start chewing. Drop through you like an anvil.

She would smile, lift the side of her mouth that way and smile with the corners of her lips, making that little curve . . .

Oh, Christ, he thought—oh Midge, I don't think I can stand this.

He slammed his hand against the side of the wagon once, and again until his knuckles bled, and he let the pain cut through the sadness. Then he picked up the sacks and made a twin-pack. In one sack he put the bacon, some cans of peaches and tomatoes, and the flour. He also put in a piece of rope and a cut-off corner of tarp that had been over the goods in the wagon. He did not have a blanket, and in any case didn't figure to sleep, but he thought if it rained he might protect the food or put the tarp piece over his shoulders to keep going.

When both bags were packed he tied them together with a short length of rope and draped them over the jack's shoulders.

The jack scooted sideways but held for it, and he took another piece of rope and went under the jack's belly with it, making a crude cinch. He could have carried the same pack in back of the saddle on the jenny, but he was big, almost too big for her, and any weight he could save would let her travel easier.

When he was done he mounted the jenny, took the jack's rope in one hand, and left. He did not hesitate, did not look back, did nothing for the wagon or the remaining goods. Somebody would come and take them or they wouldn't; the wagon could sit there and rot or get hit by lightning and burn up. It didn't matter. All that mattered were the mules and the Smith at his side, his only weapon. He checked it, spun the cylinder to make sure none of the primers were rubbing the back plate, and replaced it in the holster.

Then he aimed the jenny north along the mountains, pulled the jack into line behind, and they started moving. The jack pulled backwards a bit and shied from the weight on his back for half a mile, then he went to work and Murphy started watching ahead. He would see the dust before he saw the horses or men, would see their dust before they saw him, and it would give him time to get ready.

To his left the mountains stopped the setting sun, splattered it in golden rays across the sky, and bathed everything in a rich gold light that made even the mules seem to glow; but he paid no attention. He angled slightly left and found the tracks of the horse herd. It would be impossible to miss them, wide as a highway and churning the dirt to powder.

He tried to remember if there was a full moon but couldn't. So much had happened in the last week—he couldn't remember most of it. If there was a moon he might be able to track at night as well.

He rode in silence, though meadowlarks sang around him and there was an almost constant keening of night hawks—a high, piercing whistle sound—that came with evening as they did their evening hunts. He moved with the jenny, rolling with her walk to ease the load on her, and in an hour he got off and walked, leading her with the jack's rope tied to the saddle horn.

Darkness came. There was not a full moon, but the jenny started to have purpose in her walk and he realized she was walking the tracks on her own. She had figured out that he wanted to follow them and had taken over. She could smell the tracks in the dark and after a time he believed in her, trusted her and began to doze in the saddle.

It didn't work quite right because the saddle was too small. He could get his back end right and the front of his legs hit wrong on the fork; or he could get his legs hooked into the fork right and his hind end bounced wrong off the cantle. There was nothing more miserable than a saddle that didn't fit. But he finally caught some rest—he didn't figure on catching the riders for two or three days—and sometime in the middle of the night, with the jenny walking easily and the jack following like a sheepdog, the days and nights of madness caught up with him, hammered him with exhaustion, and Murphy fell sound asleep while riding.

He wasn't sure how long he slept, his chin bouncing down against his chest and drool running out of his mouth—perhaps two hours, a bit more—but he was awakened suddenly by the jenny stopping.

He opened his eyes. The darkness was thick, almost something to chew—he couldn't see even the jenny's head—but he sensed immediately that something was different, something was wrong. A hundred times while working the law he had sensed the same thing. In a dark alley, or the space between two buildings, there would be a smell, an evil touch to the night, a wrongness in the air. He had the same feeling now.

But the mules made no sound. If there were horses they would snuffle, perhaps bray and call. There was nothing. They had just stopped, and Murphy ran his hand up the jenny's neck and could feel that she was looking ahead at something, her huge ears forward.

The hair went up on his neck. He eased out of the saddle, keeping the mass of the jenny between him and whatever she was looking at, and pulled the Smith. He put his thumb on the hammer but did not cock it. He waited, holding his breath, trying to see-hear what was ahead.

It didn't figure to be the long riders. They would have a fire, would have the horses. But there was something wrong. Something bad.

For long moments he waited, the jenny standing quietly, looking ahead, the jack doing the same thing. When nothing moved, when no sound came, he wrapped the jenny's reins around his left hand and moved forward slowly, the Smith raised in front of him.

It had been a camp. More. It had been a camp and it had been a man and it had been a woman and the long riders had come.

Squatters moved through the country all the time, looking not for gold but for dirt. Banks in the east took the land from them and they came west—sometimes in trains of wagons, more often on the railroad—looking for dirt to farm so they could borrow money from western banks and get foreclosed on again to move on looking for more dirt. Murphy had seen them in droves. Hard-handed men with whipcord muscles who wanted only to turn the soil and plant; washed-eyed women with red skin and freckles from the sun, sitting with cages of chickens and ducks on wagons, waiting for their men in front of stores or saloons, kids swarming around them like pups in a dogyard, screaming and running.

Farmers. They would, ultimately, win—they would own and tame and break the land down. Murphy could see that. They didn't stop, they kept coming, and they would in the end hold out and win.

But not this time.

This time the farmers had lost. It looked like the riders came on them when they were camped. There was a place where a fire had been laid, a round stone fire box like the kind Midge had used when they traveled. Murphy felt the ashes and they were stone cold, dead cold, and had taken a settled dampness. Probably two days anyway. It was hard to see in the darkness, and he found some sage and a tumbleweed and started them with a match. In the sudden flare from the flames he could read what had happened.

They had shot the man outright. He lay, face down on the off side of the fire pit, fully clothed except that his boots were gone. He was head out from the fire, so they must have shot him in the back. The soles of his bare feet shone like yellow marble in the light from the burning sage.

There was the body of a small boy about ten yards further on. Perhaps ten or twelve years old. He must have tried to run because he had fallen in stride, and the way it looked he must have been hit three or four times. He was messed a bit, his legs still in an attitude of moving.

The woman they had saved for a time. She lay closer to the fire pit, nude, her body battered from use. When they'd finished with her they'd shot her in the head—one hole in her forehead as she lay face up—the damage to the back of her head hidden against the ground. Her body looked strangely young for a farm woman with a child, but her face showed both her age and the horror of what had happened.

Murphy swore and went to all three and closed their eyes. He did not feel grief—he had used all that on Midge. He did not even feel added anger or rage. He was already full of hate for the riders. But there was an angered sorrow for the farmer and his family, for Hiram sitting eating at a table in a café, for Midge—a rolling, added sorrow for all of them that seemed to fill him somehow, that gave him strength.

He closed his eyes and could see it as it must have happened. The farmer with his family, the fire, a wagon and team—the riders had taken these, as they had taken the farmer's boots—getting ready for night camp. Looking for land along the front of the mountains just as he and Midge had done.

Then, suddenly, riders. Probably three or four of them out ahead of the horse herd, drawn by the light of the fire. Riding up, shattering the night for them, gunning the man down, dropping the kid as he ran, grabbing the woman . . .

He did not have a shovel this time. Not even a hunting knife. He had the Smith and a Barlow pocketknife, and neither could be used for digging a grave. He added some bits of wood he found nearby and more sage and tumbleweed and in the light whittled a digging stick. But after an hour of clawing at the ground it was plain he would be two days digging a grave large enough for the three of them. He could ride on. They weren't his responsibility. But something in him wouldn't let him leave them like they were, open to the coyotes.

He had the bit of tarp he'd cut. He laid the three of them next to each other and covered them with the tarp, then spent the rest of the night gathering stones to cover them. It wasn't a proper grave, nothing near it, and in truth the coyotes might dig them out anyway, or a bear could wander down out of the mountains and slap the rocks away. But it was something for them. A place for them to sleep.

It was dawn when he finished and he was tired. He had no coffee—he had left it in the wagon, although he had a pan to boil water if he'd had some grounds—and there was nothing left from the farmers. The riders had taken everything.

He mounted the jenny and rode from the place without looking back. Burying, or covering, them had taken five extra hours—twenty or thirty miles if the riders had kept moving—but he felt no urgency now. They weren't scared of him, didn't know he was coming, would just keep moving normally.

And he would catch them.

He closed his eyes and dozed on the jenny, let his body roll with her walk as the sun splashed across the prairie spread out below him to the east and warmed him.

He would catch them.

CHAPTER 14

IF Murphy had held any worry about being able to follow the riders or losing their tracks, during the next six days he needn't have been concerned. It was like following a bad wind, a plague over the land.

They'd come on a small herd of cattle being driven by two hands. Murphy couldn't tell how many cattle. Fifteen or twenty or a bit more. They'd shot the hands, two young men, and taken their boots, guns, horses, even their hats. Here they'd also stopped to eat heavy. They'd killed one of the cattle and slaughtered it, cooking roasts on sticks over a fire next to the bodies of the two hands. Apparently they'd used one of the bodies for target practice, because it was shot to pieces, hit fifty or sixty times.

"Christ . . ." Murphy had mumbled, viewing the scene. "Animals." He had no tarp, the ground was too hard to dig without a shovel or pick, so he'd had to leave them for the coyotes.

But he was gaining on them. When he felt the ashes here he thought he could feel traces of warmth. If it was real, if he wasn't imagining it, that would put him perhaps ten or twelve hours in back of them. Another full night of riding while they slept.

All that day riding he watched for their dust but could see nothing. Just before dark he stopped briefly, weak with hunger. He made a small fire in a gully near a creek and cooked some bacon and ate it with a can of tomatoes, chewing woodenly, swallowing rapidly to get the food into him. He also gave the mules some oats, and he thought momentarily when he fed them that he was down to three or four pounds, but that was all right because this was the last night they'd have to move hard. Or move at all if he didn't play it right and got killed.

Stupid. Even after he got to the men and killed them he'd have to get back to the grave to end it. So four, five more days of riding before it was done. All done.

After eating, he poured water on the fire and started riding again, looking for fire. They'd surely build a fire. They'd shown no caution so far, there was no reason for it now. But he rode the whole night along the range seeing no light.

Somewhere in the middle of the night, perhaps one or two in the morning, the jenny tried to head off to the right. They had been riding along the range, north by a little west—he kept the Dipper on the right side of his face—and the jenny worked in a large curve once while he dozed so she was heading almost straight east, down the long, gradual incline that led out into the prairie. Horses and mules would do that, he knew, work down a hill if left to their own devices because it was easier to move that way.

But the jenny hadn't done it in all these miles. It was strange that she chose to do it now. He brought her head back to the northwest and they started again, but twice more she tried it before settling back to work. He thought the trail might move off that way, but when he got off and used a match to light the ground, the wide band of horse tracks seemed to keep to the northwest.

"Just moving downhill," he mumbled to himself, after a bit. Left to its own devices a horse will work downhill.

He remounted and kept her moving northwest and soon had forgotten it.

Dawn caught him dozing and brought a sudden frost. The ground was white with it, some of the standing sage and tumbleweeds looked like ice webs, and he saw the steam out of the jenny's nostrils, felt the cold in his legs and arms. It surprised him. The days were scalding hot. But it was August and coming toward fall, and he was at the edge of the mountains, high enough for early frost; and an edge of his thinking was wondering about the frost, how fast the summer had gone, when he realized there were no tracks in front of him.

He stopped the jenny and swore.

How long, he thought—how long had they been moving without tracks? He raised in the stirrups, looking ahead and down to the right, but he could see no sign.

So the jenny had been right. They had moved off to the east, and he had ridden past where they turned like a damn fool, ignoring the jenny and pulling her north.

Damn.

He looked back, half expecting to see something, but it was still early light—a gray light that seemed to wash everything in a pale glow—and he could not see more than three or four hundred yards before things faded. In the night they had moved into some light break country, choppy gullies that cut deep as they came out of the mountains but quickly widened into dry riverbeds as they moved out into the plains.

He turned the jenny and started back and down, watching for where they had cut off. It could be miles. If the jenny had been right, it might be six or seven miles to where they had turned east. There must have been a slight breeze and she caught the smell of the herd below them before they actually got to the place the riders had turned. And he had made her move away. They had been close there.

Really close to them. He felt his stomach tighten with it, thinking of them there, just below him in the prairie. They may have been stopped in a riverbed with a low fire, which would keep him from seeing the flames or glow.

So he'd have to make up the distance he'd gone off the trail, then catch up with them. He stopped for a moment, letting the new sun warm him. His hands were stiff on the reins and the heat from the sun loosened them. If he rode back and then down it could take many hours. But if he cut across the angle and down he could save time. Might even run up on them. They'd still be moving slowly, not worrying.

He angled the jenny down, heading now southeast, and started moving again. In half an hour he had good light though he was still cold. The temperature seemed to drop just at dawn. He could see the whole of the prairie spread out below him and there was no dust, no sign of movement.

The sun warmed him and he rode for an hour loosely, fighting the sleep that seemed always ready to take him, and it was in this state, half dozing and letting the sun cut the night off him, that he rode up on the two men.

The jenny gave him half a second warning but it wasn't enough, and at any rate he didn't see it in time to do anything. Perhaps if he weren't so tired, or acting normally, he would have been able to react. But it all happened   so fast . . .

They were working through one of the dozens of dry riverbeds that snaked out of the mountains down onto the prairie. This time it was a narrow bed, cut deep by spring runoff though bone dry now. He slid the jenny down one side, dragging the jack after him, and once in the bottom he saw that the other side was too steep to climb out. He would have to ride downstream a bit and find a more sloping bank.

He turned the jenny, started down the bed, and hadn't gone two hundred feet when he came to a blind corner. The jenny kept plodding, but he noticed one ear suddenly snap forward as if pulled on a string, and he felt her muscles quicken beneath him—and at the same instant two men came riding around the corner.

All in part of a second things happened. He recognized them as two of the riders he'd seen in Casper. It slashed into his brain. One younger man and one older. For the smallest part of an instant time froze. He stared at them, they stared at him. Then there was a wild flurry of movement.

"Goddam," one of them said, getting half the word out and grabbing for his gun. The other one was older and didn't waste time swearing. His hand pulled a Colt's out of a cross-draw rig with practiced ease.

Perhaps because he was tired, or maybe because he'd been torn apart by the past week of his life—whatever the reason—Murphy made just about every mistake he could. His cold fingers were still a bit stiff, but he managed to claw the Smith out and get the hammer back. Yet like an amateur he swung on the young one first, because he was a bit closer, and fired. He hit solidly enough, somewhere high and right in the man's chest. He saw the dust puff off his shirt and he fired a second shot double-action, trying to get something into the second man, anything to stop him—but it was too late.

The second man fired the Colt's as Murphy's Smith

recoiled. He had never been good at double action, and his bullet went wide and to the right, but it wouldn't have mattered. The Colt's bullet caught him solidly in the left shoulder, high and left on his chest, and the impact swung him around and almost took him off the jenny. Fighting pain and the dizziness that comes with getting hit, Murphy pulled the Smith back around and fired twice as fast as he could.

The first of his bullets missed the rider, who was in the act of pulling off a second shot. Murphy was wheeling around to the left and it saved his life. The man's bullet would have taken him square in the chest, but because he was turning it caught him along his right side—Murphy thought he could actually hear a rib break with the hit—tearing a path through the right side of his chest.

In the same instant his second bullet caught the rider just under the left eye, taking the brain and killing him instantly, the force of the hit taking him up and back in the saddle.

All of this happened in less than two seconds—recognition, movement, an almost tearing sound of gunfire, the shots so close together it was impossible to separate them—and in the same two seconds the jenny went insane.

Murphy's first shot went right between her ears and the muzzle blast of the Smith nearly took her eardrums out. No horse likes to be shot from—though they could be trained to take it—and nobody had ever shot from the jenny or even close to her. The sudden concussion and roar of the Smith coming in the quiet morning, just as she saw the horses of the two riders, was enough to cause the jenny to explode.

By Murphy's third shot she was turning and he

grabbed the horn to keep from falling. Strangely, he hadn't felt shock from the second bullet hitting him— his body seemed to have concentrated on the first one in the shoulder—but the pain from both of the hits began to grow as the jenny wheeled.

He made a sound, some low sound in his throat with the pain, and dropped the Smith and hung onto the horn as she turned and started running up the riverbed. The jolting of movement made the broken ends of his ribs grate and moved the ends of something in the shoulder wound as well, and he almost screamed with the pain.

There was a slash of something red through his brain, some hot red cutting jagged edge of searing pain, and he could not think more, could form no thoughts except to hang onto the horn as the jenny bolted; and by the time she had dropped to a trot, then to a fast walk, still moving up the dry riverbed, he was little more than meat on her back.

The shock of the two wounds had taken him. His eyes were open but unseeing, his hands, obeying some instinctive command from his brain, held onto the horn with a near deathgrip, but there was nothing left of him.

The jenny carried him, walking as she'd walked for days, happy to be away from the noise of the guns, carrying him back toward the mountains.

CHAPTER 15

FOR a time there was nothing. Not even pain. He knew nothing, felt nothing, was nothing.

Then there were dreams. They came with the riding, the endless riding, as he fought to hang onto the horn.

Childhood dreams. He dreamt of the Tenderloin in New York and his mother bringing men home to their cheap crib-room in the grubby tenement and the men paying her—endless streams of men who would give him nickels and smile and pat his head or cuff him out of the way like a stray dog. And the recruiter who talked him into heading west with the army in a "grand quest for adventure." The goddam recruiter was there. In the dreams. Talking to his mother and giving her money and taking the boy who was not a man to send him west and clean stables and fight. Then it all mixed in the dreams so that his mother became the recruiter and the recruiter became a whore and they all talked to him, told him to hang onto the saddle horn and keep riding, keep riding.

He thought he rode for a long time, but it could have been only a short distance and the dreams made it long, or it could have been a very long distance and the dreams were real. He could not know.

Sun. He remembered sun on his back. The heat from it. And pain. Not pain he was used to, not just pain from the wounds, but pain from within. It was as if the two wounds opened a floodgate of pain so that it came in layers, pain piled on pain until the whole center of his being, his entire body and brain, screamed with it; and he thought he may have actually screamed then, or made some sound and kept making sound, because he thought he kept hearing a small cry.

At some point in the day, at some instant in the rest of his life, it became too much and he let go the saddle horn, let go of everything and fell from the jenny. He knew he fell because the jolt of hitting the ground made the broken ribs move and grate against one another and the pain intensified enough to make him completely unconscious again. He fell like a sack of grain and did not move after he hit the ground, but dropped into the sand and dirt and would have died that way, died and bled out, except that after a time one eye opened, the eye that wasn't in the dirt opened, and Midge was there.

She was wearing a dress and the light was in back of her head but it was her. She was smiling gently and leaning over him and the hair, the loose hair, hung down at the side of her face. He wanted to say her name, wanted to reach up and push the hair back as he used to do, but nothing worked any longer. *She leaned forward with care in her eyes, wiped his forehead with something, a damp rag.* He tried to grab her, hold her, keep her, but she vanished in a cloud, a mist, and the pain returned and then again everything ceased to be.

Nothing.

Some sound came through.

It was an ugly sound, a high croaking or keening, cracking sound, like a shovel being pushed into gravel and water. It cut through his blankness and was the first thing to tell him he was still alive. Second came the pain.

Not sharp as before, but waves of it floating out of his

chest and up into his head and back. It did not make him scream, but it did not let him think either. Between the waves he knew the sound, but when the pain surged he knew nothing but pain. Then he found it was his breathing. When he took air in the pain exploded. He tried not to breathe, but that only made it worse, and when the next breath came he became unconscious again.

Light. Colors. Around him an awful smell and the same keening sound he'd heard before. It all happened at once. He became aware of intense light and splashing pink colors, and after a second he realized he was seeing sunlight through his closed eyelids.

He opened his eyes and was immediately blinded by the sun. He closed them, hesitated, and opened them again, squinting. He could not move his head, could not even turn it sideways, could not move anything but his eyes.

As soon as his eyes opened the keening sound stopped. He looked sideways as much as possible without moving his head and saw the edge of a face. It was an old face, an old Indian woman's face, and he thought he knew it; but when he closed his eyes and blinked and opened them it was gone.

Then, suddenly, it was over him, shading out the sun. The face smiled and only two teeth showed. The face said something, but it was only a croaking sound to him.

Something was being held to his mouth. An edge of a thing and he realized it was a cup. He tried to turn away but the cup tipped and fluid wet his lips. It was water and he was immediately overcome with thirst. His throat, his mouth, were powder dry, crack-dry. He gulped and swallowed and immediately choked and threw up on himself.

The heaving moved his chest and the bones grated and the pain exploded and he passed out once more. But this time only for a few moments. When he came to again he could hear more—birds somewhere near, a meadowlark, a clear-clean sound. Then a snort and some words in a language he didn't understand— though he knew it was Indian—and a short laugh. He tried to see to the side by swiveling his eyes again, saw only sand and a gully wall, then turned his head.

He could move it only slowly and with great pain in the neck muscles. He was a weak, sick-weak, shot-weak. As his head swung over he saw the top of the old woman's head, then her face, then a fire, and sitting next to her at the fire an old Indian man. They both looked familiar, and after a second he realized they were the same old couple who had told them about the canyon. His mouth opened but no words came out. It was too dry and his throat had somehow tightened.

"So it was this way," the old man said suddenly, speaking to him but looking down into the fire, as if telling a story to a child. "My woman and me are getting old so we thought we'd come and winter with you and your woman in the sweet grass canyon and stay warm by your fire. It was the least you could do for us, after we told you of the canyon. We thought you might have bacon and the sweet powder. My woman likes bacon with sweet powder on it."

He took a breath and a sip of something from a tin cup. There was a pot on the fire, blackened and old, with some liquid bubbling in it. Murphy thought he should be able to smell it, the steam from it, but could smell nothing. Lord, he thought, Lord I hurt. Midge. Midge, I hurt.

"We got to that canyon all right," the old man continued. "We found that canyon like there was a string to it and we found the wagon you left and all that flour you threw on the ground—why is it white men waste so much food?—and your cabin there and the small fence white men like to make and the lean-to, and we found your woman's grave. At first I thought it was not for her, but my woman said it was too small for you because you are big. Then too your tracks and those of the other men were fresher than those we found of your woman so we thought she had died and you had gone from that place."

Another noisy slurp of liquid. This time the woman rose from the fire and brought a cup to Murphy as well and he tried to drink. It was a meat broth but tasted mostly of blood and a little salt. He held it down and wanted another drink, but the woman turned away before he could make it known.

"If you drink too fast you will throw it up again," the old man said. "So we did not want to stay in that place either and we rode out. We saw the tracks of all the horses heading up along the mountains and I thought you were driving them alone so we worked that way. I'm not sure why we did that thing. I think it was in my head that if we caught up to you, you might have some bacon and sweet powder even if you were alone and it was as good a way to go as any. It does not matter as much which way you go when you are old as it does when you are young."

The woman interrupted, said something rapidly, waited.

"My woman says she has to change the packing on your holes. It will hurt and she does not want you to strike her. If you strike her, she will leave them and you will die because the poison will drain back into you."

"I . . . won't . . ." He thought he spoke, but he heard no sound but a cracked whisper.

The woman came to him and he looked down past his nose and was surprised to see he had no shirt on. His chest and stomach were covered with dried blood.

"It is where the bullets go in that causes trouble. When they come out they carry bad things with them, but where they go in they take dirt in with them. I learned that from the goddam bluecoats. Once the goddam bluecoats came to my village and shot eight or ten people for fun and rode away. They used those big rifles which leave a hole bigger than your fist, but even so not all the people died right away. Some lived for days, but the meat got bad where the bullets went in and they died. It smelled like old buffalo. She had to pick pieces of your shirt out of the holes."

Murphy had been lulled by his talk, the endless words of it. Just then the old woman pulled some kind of packing—he thought grass and dirt mixed—from the shoulder wound. She had pushed some of it down into the bullet hole and when she pulled it out he screamed. He could no more have stopped the scream than he could turned the day to night. It wasn't just pain this time, not only pain but a blast of something more; as if she'd pushed a red hot poker through his chest.

He lost consciousness briefly again, then came up to find her putting fresh packing on both wounds and the old man still talking.

"We came on the place where you buried the three people and then came to the bodies of two riders and I thought you were killing all these people and decided to change and go some other way. But my woman is better at tracks than me and she said you were following other men who had done these things and that we should keep after you because when you caught them you would kill them and there would be many things for us to get. Maybe bacon and the sweet powder."

Murphy closed his eyes, listening but not caring. Things were all hazy, not real. He remembered seeing Midge and the peace that seeing her had brought; the quiet peace.

"My woman saw where you split off from the main track and said we should follow you. I said no, that we should go on our own way and find some buffalo to shoot and get ready for a winter. My bones feel a long winter coming. But my woman was right and we followed you. Your tracks were crazy. You went past them and on and we thought we'd lost you, but then my woman saw crows flying and we went to that place where the crows were. Her eyes are better than mine. I think it is because she is younger than me. That's where you were. In that place where the crows were we found you on the ground. There were two mules with you and you had bled all over one mule and the ground and it was the blood that draws crows. I used to think it was the smell of dead meat that brings them but it isn't. It's the smell of blood."

Murphy remembered everything then. The two men, the quick ripple of surprised gunfire. He licked his lips. "There were two men," he whispered. "I killed two men . . ."

The old man took a long slurp of soup, motioned to the woman who brought the cup to Murphy's mouth again, and shook his head. "I do not know of the two men you killed. When we found you we put you on the travois and my woman rode the small mule and we came away from that place up into the hills. Did you know you cannot ride the big mule? I tried and he bit me for my troubles. I was going to shoot him but my woman said he might be a favorite of yours and you would be mad if I shot him. Would you be mad if I shot him?"

Murphy said nothing. Tried to think.

"We saw dust out in the flat places," the old man continued. "A high cloud of it later in the day, but it was moving the other way—to the north and back out into the grass country—and we did not want to meet any people who would put two holes in you anyway so we let it go. Was that your horses, the dust?"

They must not have come looking for the two riders, Murphy thought. Just figured they'd catch up later. Or maybe they had been hunting and were expected to be gone two or three days. Or maybe—more likely the case—the rest of the riders just didn't give a damn about them, or each other.

Which meant the bodies of the two men were probably still there.

And their guns. He needed guns. If he lived he needed guns. There were six, seven of them left. He needed weapons.

"If you follow my tracks back from where you found me the bodies should still be there," he said. The old man had to come from the fire and lean over him to hear. Murphy's voice was getting weaker and he had to fight to keep from going under again. "I need the guns. Bring me the guns . . ."

And he slipped sideways, down a long slide into the quiet again.

CHAPTER 16

WHEN he next opened his eyes it was dark. He was instantly awake and alert and felt strangely rested. The pain had subsided to a sharp throb, still chewing at him but controllable, and it did not make him suck in his breath.

The woman was sitting at the fire, sipping from a cup and looking down into the flames. The glow reflected in her face highlighted it and took years off it. She still looked old, but not as old as she had and not so used by the weather and time. There was great peace in her face as she watched the fire, and he thought if I live—he was not at all sure he would, judging by the smell from his wounds—if I live it is because of her. What a strange mother she makes for me. He saw she had high cheekbones and that her eyes slanted up at the corners and lifted her cheeks, and he thought she must have been beautiful when she was young.

The old man was not in sight. And considering the quiet he must either be asleep or gone. If he'd been there he would be talking.

The inside of his mouth was dry, felt cracked, and he knew his lips were bleeding. The thirst owned him and he made some sound—tried to ask for water—and the woman looked at him.

"Water . . ." he hissed.

She laughed and said something he could not understand—her voice sounded like air pushed through

117

cloth—and came to squat next to him. She held the same cup she had been drinking from to his lips and he drank greedily, almost choking when he found it wasn't water but the same blood broth he had tasted earlier. He fought to hold it down, did so, and she went back to the fire and refilled the cup from the pot there and returned to his side.

Again she made a sound he could not understand and held the cup to his lips. He guessed she was telling him to drink, and he got most of the second cup down before turning away.

"You have lost a lot of blood." The old man suddenly appeared, walking up to the fire with his arms full of belts, holsters, and rifles. "That is juice from buffalo liver heated up. We shot a buffalo three days ago and you're lucky she saved part of the liver to make the juice for you. It will make new blood for you." He dumped the guns and belts in the dirt next to the fire. "I found those two men you killed. One was where he fell off the horse, but the other had crawled ten or twelve paces before he died. Both horses were eating nearby. We are rich—with two more horses and all their guns, and one of them had tobacco in his pocket with only a little blood on it. And their gun belts are only a small bit chewed by the coyotes." He reached under his shirt and pulled out another gun. "And I found your gun where it fell from your hands as I was riding back."

He brought the Smith to Murphy, who took it in his hand. He was so weak that the weight of it made it fall to his lap. He broke open the top and ejected the three empty cartridges that he had fired during the fight. Fight hell, he thought, half snorting and wincing with the pain the sudden movement made—more like a disaster.

He raised his head and tried to look around the fire. "Where's my gun belt?"

The old man said something to the woman and she got up, went to a blanket roll, and brought him the belt and holster. He took three cartridges from the belt, shook each one next to his ear to make sure the powder was loose—a trick he'd learned after having a box of defective cartridges damn near kill him because moisture had gotten into them and ruined the powder—and reloaded the gun. He rotated the cylinder to make sure it worked freely, then put the gun back in the holster and laid it by his side.

For once the old man had been silent, watching him work with the gun. "It is part of you—the gun. You are one of those who make their living with guns."

It was a statement, not a question, and Murphy said nothing. Looked at the fire.

"Are you the same as those men you follow?"

Murphy looked up. "No. I was the law in a town called Cincherville. I quit because I was sick of it. We were going to raise horses but those men came and . . ." He let it slide off. It wasn't necessary to speak.

The old man squatted and warmed his hands by the fire. There was a chill in the air, a cutting edge. Fall was close, winter coming. "You are going after those men again . . ."

Once more it was not a question, and Murphy said nothing.

"For what they did to your woman."

Murphy stared into the fire.

"I have not made war in a long time and I miss it. Perhaps I will help you."

Now Murphy looked up. "No. They will just kill you."

"I am not so easy to kill. I am not the one lying with

two holes while my woman pours liver juice down his throat to make blood."

Murphy smiled at that. "That's true. But this isn't your fight."

"I am old. This might be my last chance to make a little war. I used to love war when I was young. Once I fought three Crow and counted coup on all of them and twice I have killed white men." He hesitated, looking at Murphy. "They were bad white men, of course."

Murphy nodded. "Of course. I have done the same thing. With the bad ones."

"Yes." The old man squatted by the fire and nodded. "I think I will help you. It will be a good fight."

No, Murphy thought—it won't. But he didn't say anything. The old man had made his mind up and there was nothing further to say.

He closed his eyes and slept—only this time it truly was sleep and not passing out, smelling his wounds.

He awakened to bright daylight, not just dawn but high morning.

The woman was at the fire, singing. Or he guessed it was singing. She had a large pot going now and had something boiling in water. The steam came across him and the smell was so good it made his mouth water. A rich meat smell with something else, something else— his wound. The wound smell was gone.

He raised his head weakly—it seemed to be too heavy for his neck—and examined his wounds. The packing was gone, and with it the stink of rot, and she had covered the holes with pieces of cloth to keep the flies out. The cloth was clean—she must have washed the rags in hot water from the fire—and he raised the one on his shoulder to find the bullet hole covered over with pink, fleshy tissue. He could not see where the bullets came out but he knew, as the old man had said, that exit wounds healed faster than where the bullets went in. He knew about bullet wounds.

The old man suddenly appeared in front of him, squatting. "She is making a stew with some buffalo, some grass she likes, and some of what you call prairie dogs in it. I could never understand why white men called them dogs when they are nothing like dogs and do not taste like dogs, but I think it is like names. White men have names that don't mean anything. What is your name?"

"Murphy."

"There. You see? That means nothing. You should be named something that means a thing. The Big Man Who Kills. I, for instance, am named Woman Chaser for something that happened in my youth. I was in my fourteenth summer and on a raid against the Crows, but they left me to hold the horses . . ."

And he was off once more. Murphy closed his eyes and let the story move over him, and in moments he was asleep again.

This time when he woke it was early morning and he was starved. Not just hungry and thirsty, but starved. He rolled on his side—the pain was little more than a dull, quick nudge—and tried to pull himself toward the pot on the cold fire. But as soon as he moved the woman was there and dipped a cup into the stew and handed it to him.

He swallowed it almost in a single draught, handed it back, and she refilled it and he drained it again, tasting it this time. It was a rich stew, the meat cooked to shreds, with a taste of sage in it and the fine meat of the prairie dogs mixing with the coarser textured meat of buffalo.

"It's good." Murphy smiled. "All very good . . ."

She said nothing, took the cup, and moved away.

"We'll be moving today," the old man said—he had a disconcerting habit of appearing just out of Murphy's vision suddenly. "We have been here too long—here six, no seven days now . . ."

"Seven days!" Murphy said. "That can't be. I counted two or three . . ."

"No. It is seven. You slept all of three days, almost four days, crying like a baby at night. *Tscha!*" He laughed like a horse snorting. "My woman had to help you like a child when you needed to relieve yourself. You don't remember that?"

Seven days, Murphy thought. They had a seven-day lead now. Seventy, eighty miles. "You're right. We have to start moving down country. Help me get up."

This brought cackles from the old man, who explained something to the woman, and they both laughed.

"You think you will ride?"

"Help me," Murphy said. "Please."

He rolled to his knees—pain now rising in both wounds—and tried to raise himself. He couldn't. He hung there, half up, weak, dizzy, everything rolling and swaying.

"We will put you on the travois." The old Indian stepped forward and took him by his good shoulder. "Maybe after a day or so you can try to stand. You must not hurry this or you will fall and start bleeding again."

Murphy shook his head. "Goddammit, help me to my feet." All he knew of wounds and injuries told him that the sooner he could walk, could move and use his body, the faster it would heal. "I'll ride the travois some, but let me walk to it. Let me move around first."

They moved so there was one on each side of him, like living crutches—they barely came up to his armpits—and pulled him up.

He swayed like a tree about to fall and nearly yelled with the stretching of the tissue around the wounds. But he held that way for a moment, on the edge of collapse, then took a step. He did almost fall, and they had to hold him up, but the second step was easier and he felt the stew he'd eaten flow into his body. Before he got to the horse waiting with the travois he was walking alone—tottering, weaving, but walking alone.

Seven days. He thought suddenly of Doc back in Cincherville. He'd never believe it. Pack grass in wounds and drink raw liver blood and you're on your feet in seven days.

He sat on the edge of the travois. The old lady would ride the jenny, the jack was still following, and the old man would ride the travois horse. They would lead the other two horses with a rope tied to the travois. He'd rigged a pack on one of them to carry all the gear and the rifles and handguns and a chunk of buffalo meat they still had that "only smelled a little."

The old man was right, Murphy thought.

He was rich.

CHAPTER 17

THEY didn't make five miles before Murphy was out of the travois. He had been more or less woven into the load with the stew pot and bedrolls around him, but the thing rode like a wagon with square wheels; every rock and bump and chuckhole slammed up into him through the poles and he was in very real danger of having his wounds open up.

He signaled the old woman to give him the jenny and she clambered down. She'd been riding in Midge's saddle, but he's lengthened the stirrups so her feet didn't get down to them, and the stirrups flapped as she rode. She didn't seem to mind losing the jenny and was on the travois in three steps, sitting staring backwards as the old man clucked the pony into motion.

Murphy pulled himself onto the jenny, weaving with it. He was weak and his muscles felt almost runny, but he held and she was good enough about it—he was developing a fondness for her and wondered what would happen to her after it was all over.

They started off again at a walk—he wouldn't be able to trot or canter for some time—and he balanced and went into a kind of doze. He lost measure of time and place, knew only the travois skidding along in front of him and the sun on his face and the endless drone of the old man talking, talking, talking as they moved slowly down, out into the prairie.

Sometime in the middle of that first day the old

woman called a halt and motioned for him to get down. She examined the wounds and neither nodded nor shook her head, but he thought she felt pleased about them, and she made him drink some of the broth and eat the meat she had brought in a covered pot on the travois. He drank until he was done, but she made him drink more, until he thought he was going to throw up and had to fight to hold it down.

That satisfied her and she put the pot back on the travois.

Murphy felt immediate strength when he drank and ate. It was like pouring fuel oil on a fire. He climbed back on the jenny—already gaining strength—and they rode the rest of the day.

Toward mid-afternoon he moved to the lead. There was nothing said or meant by it. He was riding in back of the travois, slightly to the side to avoid the rope behind the horses that was tied to the travois poles, and he rode up alongside the old man.

"We have to talk," Murphy said.

In truth the old man had not stopped talking for ten seconds since they had started to ride. He told endless tales of war, of raids to steal horses or women or guns, long-reaching tales of rides that covered territories, of winds that blew through a man, of monster cold and monster heat and fights and wounds and blood, and Murphy was convinced that they were all lies. But it didn't matter because they were good stories.

"I am strong enough now to ride alone," Murphy said. "Thank you for saving me, but it's best if I work this alone."

"*Tscha!*" The old man blew his nose with his finger. "They will just kill you when you catch up with them.

You can't do it alone. Why not save the time and trouble and shoot yourself?"

Murphy said nothing for a time. It was late afternoon and he felt the sun on his back and the heat on the wounds felt good. Like warm ointment. "This has nothing to do with you," he said. "These men are nothing to you."

The old man sighed. "It is as I said—it's a good fight. Plus we may get more horses and guns. I can sell the horses and take the guns back to some people I know who will give me a warm bed and fresh meat all winter for them. No, I think we will follow you."

Murphy gave up and pulled the jenny ahead, settling back into riding.

They cut the tracks again later in the day. It hadn't rained since before he was shot, since before he returned to find Midge, and the tracks where the herd of horses chewed the ground with their hooves and grazed left a wide highway to follow.

They cut back from the north until they were heading not just east but a little south. On their original track they would have hit Deadwood in the Black Hills, and this new direction puzzled Murphy.

"There's nothing there—the direction they're going." Murphy stopped the jenny. "Except for the flat country out in South Dakota."

"You're wrong," the old man said. He scratched and spit. "My woman and me were out there a year and a half ago and there is a town on the south end of the Black Hills where those hot holes in the ground boil out. The white men call the place Hot Springs. Those men are probably going to sell the horses there."

Murphy started again, riding down the chewed swath well into darkness, and he would have ridden all night except that twice he lost the trail in the dark—there was no moon yet—and he finally had to admit to a stop. "We can build a fire and stop for three or four hours, rest the stock and eat."

"You ride like a crazy person," the old man said, raising his leg and sliding sideways off the travois horse. "Even with two holes in you, you ride like a crazy person. If we do not find them in two days, we will in three— why do you hurry to die?"

Murphy said nothing. He dismounted stiffly. The wounds hadn't opened, and they were still healing. But they had stiffened and he hung on the side of the jenny for a moment and gathered his strength. When he had his feet he pulled the saddle and bridle but tied a long rope to her halter and knotted it to a willow. The old man did the same with the travois horse. The woman had a fire going and two pots cooking on it seemingly before Murphy could dismount. In minutes there was water boiling and hot stew and they ate and drank in silence, except of course for the old man.

Then they wrapped themselves in bedrolls, the old man and woman together in one and Murphy in the other, and dozed on their sides next to the fire as it died, sleeping on and off until Murphy caught the first gray of dawn cutting the eastern edge of the prairie—it seemed like only an hour but was close to four—when he got up. He stretched gingerly, until pain stopped the movement. He could use his right arm and shoulder fairly well, the left was still close to useless, and if he moved too fast or far his ribs felt as if somebody were turning a knife in his side.

He moved quietly, hoping to get away, but the old man was awake, watching him as he lit a fire to heat water. Even without coffee, hot water in the morning seemed to help start things.

"You have to get another woman," he said, studying Murphy carefully. "To keep you warm when it snaps cold like this . . ."

"No. I don't," Murphy said flatly, and the old man dropped it.

Using his right arm, Murphy pulled the jenny up and put the blanket and saddle over her. He left the cinch loose for a moment while he took the water off the fire and drank a cup as hot and fast as he could, feeling it scald his tongue. The heat moved into his limbs.

The old man scrambled up and the woman grumbled a bit and followed.

"Women do not like war as much as men," he explained, his breath coming out in steam. There was fall close in the air now. "She would rather stay in the blankets until the sun warms her bones."

Murphy didn't answer, tightened the cinch, and mounted. He was moving more easily all the time, and he turned the jenny's big ears east and started riding, settling his weight into the saddle as she began walking. The saddle was still too small, and he had the larger saddles from the horses of the two men he'd killed, but he couldn't change somehow; there was Midge in the saddle, some memory of her, and he couldn't put the saddle aside even if it didn't fit.

He rode into morning. Birds rose around him, meadowlarks sang, hawks keened, the sky splashed a blue explosion over him—and he saw none of it, saw nothing but the tracks out ahead of him. He rode down the middle of them, his face even, his eyes straight ahead, the old man and woman and jack and horses trailed out in back of him in a scraggly line, and Murphy paid no attention to any of them.

Just the tracks. He rode in silence, working his left hand and arms slowly, squeezing a fist, releasing it, squeezing it, raising the arm and letting it down.

Just the tracks.

CHAPTER 18

IT wouldn't be right to call Hot Springs a town, as the old man had said. It was more a blister. An ugly carbuncle stuck on a flat place in the middle of nowhere. Wood buildings more or less stuck together in a group that formed a settlement but without order or sense. There were two saloons, a livery with a large corral out to the side of the settlement, three wooden huts that must have been dwellings but were little more than slab hovels, five or six tattered canvas tents where the owners couldn't afford wood—and all of it, all of it stinking of horse and human waste.

Hot Springs.

Murphy pulled the jenny up on a low hill a quarter of a mile west of town and studied it. Three days of hard travel to get here, he thought, and it was no place to get to, at least no place good. Over one of the saloons—just a rough-sawn wood building with holes big enough to throw a cat through—a wooden shutter slammed open and a woman nude from the waist up threw a bucket of dirty water out of the window and down the side of the building. She hesitated for a moment, seeing Murphy but not covering herself, then slammed the shutter closed.

There was a herd of horses and cattle in the corral. Murphy didn't count them, but even from this distance he could make out the gelding and he recognized several of the others. The cattle must have belonged to the two dead riders.

"Those are the horses," the old man said, riding up next to him. The woman still sat on the travois, but when the old man stopped she jumped off and brought him a rifle after working the lever to make sure there was a shell in the chamber.

Murphy pulled the Smith and checked the loads, then put it back in the holster. Then he reached back and untied a sack that had been tied to the cantle. He opened it and pulled out a Colt's the old man had taken off one of the dead men. Murphy had worked on it during the ride, cleaning it with the corner of his shirt as the jenny walked, oiling it with a bit of buffalo fat the old woman gave him until the hammer worked easily and the cylinder turned loosely. He checked the Colt's one more time to make sure it was full—with not even an empty one under the hammer—and stuck it in his belt. He thought briefly of spare shells for the Colt's but decided against it. It took .45 longs, a different cartridge from his Smith, which took a .44, and if he couldn't get the job done in twelve shots he probably wouldn't be alive anyway.

He got off the jenny and stood with her body between him and town. "One more time—you don't want any of this." He looked up at the old man, who dismounted as he spoke. "There's isn't but one way this can go . . ."

The old man smiled. "Can I have that fancy gun of yours if you die and I live? The one that breaks at the top?"

Murphy said nothing, but turned back to the town. The sun was almost directly overhead, which probably didn't matter. They were in the saloons or the cribs, drinking and whoring. Figure five or six of them. Plus any others who got excited and threw in with them once it started.

He started walking, leading the jenny. Once he got her moving he hung back a bit, so he could step in back of her and use her for a shield if need be, and he moved steadily into town. The old man said something to the woman in Indian, then followed him, but far enough back so the jenny already covered him. Murphy knew he was there without turning.

He reached the front of the first saloon without incident, dropped the reins, and stepped up and in the door, moving out of the light to the side as soon as he was in. The old man hung back.

Two men at the bar, neither of them recognizable, turned to see him come in, then went back to drinking. A bartender paused in cleaning his nails with a clasp knife but went back to it.

Three more men sat at a table with a bottle. One of them had a dark suit on with dust at the elbows, and Murphy didn't know him. The other two seemed familiar, and for a heartbeat he hesitated.

Then one of them looked up and saw him and Murphy saw his eyes go wide. "Casper. It's the one from Casper . . ."

Murphy had the Smith out. He shot the man, holding on the chest but pulling high and hitting him in the throat. He went back and down as if struck with a hammer, and before he hit the floor Murphy had pulled twice more and the other man was hit through the hips, crawling away.

There was a tremendous roar, and smoke filled the room and the man crawling on the floor was driven sideways, his chest blown open. Murphy turnd to see the old Indian in the door with the rifle, working the lever.

"He was still moving."

A moment of silence. The bartender had jerked when the firing started and cut his finger. He sucked on it, watching Murphy and the Smith as he'd look at a snake. The man in the dusty suit hadn't moved. Both his hands were on the table, palms down. "I'm out of this," he said. "I'm a horse buyer."

"Are there any more in here?"

"No. There are three more over at Jerkies—that's the other saloon. Would this have anything to do with that herd of horses and cattle out there?"

"Partly."

"Damn. I just bought them."

"You can get your money back in a bit."

"Or what's left of it," the buyer said ruefully. "They've been spending for ten, twelve hours."

"Is that how many men came with the horses—five?"

"Yes."

Murphy backed out of the door and into the street again. Three more and he hadn't seen the leader yet. It didn't matter. Which one didn't matter. He was cold with it, cold and flat with it—no feeling came with killing them. He was shooting rabid dogs. He broke the Smith and popped the three empties out, replaced them and closed it, rotated the cylinder to free it, and stepped out into the sun.

All of this hadn't taken half a minute, and as he moved down the street—or open area, there was very little street to it—a man appeared out of the other saloon and stood on the slab porch, partially hidden by a vertical post. It was a good fifty yards, too far for a handgun, but the man raised his and fired twice rapidly. Both shots went wide to the right. Murphy heard them go past and was sighting his own to answer the fire and at least throw the man's aim off when the old man's rifle bellowed again to his right, nearly taking his eardrum out. A chunk of wood splintered off the support just above the shooter's head and the old Indian swore.

"I'm shooting high. It's because I'm old. My eyes see things wrong."

When the rifle slug hit the post the man jumped back into the saloon, and for another fifteen seconds there was silence.

"They're getting ready for us," Murphy said. "They're getting settled in . . ."

Just then the saloon door exploded open and four men came running out and across the street between two buildings. One of the men had an apron on. The old man started to raise the rifle but Murphy pushed the barrel down. "It's just customers and the bartender—getting out."

"We could wait and when they got hungry they would come out."

"No. I'm not waiting for them."

"I did not think so."

"I'm going to go in the back way," Murphy said. "There's a back door leading to the outhouse. You can stay out here and watch the front and if any come out, either before or after, kill them. You understand what I'm saying?"

He nodded. "You want me to kill them."

"If I'm alive or if I'm dead, it makes no matter. You kill them anyway. I'll give you those horses in the corral. Don't let those bastards live."

"I could go in with you . . ."

"No. This is insurance. Even if I get put down, you take them when they come out. And make sure they are dead, like the man in the saloon. Shoot them all twice."

"You must hate these men."

"Yes."

He left the old man then and crossed the street to get to the back of the saloon. On the side of the building were written the words DRINKING EMPORIUM, but they couldn't lend any dignity to the building. It had been made of green lumber, with bats covering the cracks, and between warping and twisting it looked like the peeling dead skin of a leper.

Murphy trotted to the back of the building, surprised that he hadn't drawn fire. They must see me, he thought, how can they not see me? But he made the rear of the saloon and stood next to the door. Force of habit made him check the Smith again and resettle the Colt's in his belt so it was ready to grab. Then he took four pulled, deep breaths, wincing with the rib pain—it seemed to sharpen him to breathe deeply—held the Smith in both hands, kicked the door, and rolled in and down to the left, not falling so much as sliding off down the wall, the Smith ready in front of him.

The doorway was hammered with bullets. He saw two men in the saloon in back of the board bar ready for him, but they misjudged and thought he would come straight in, and they fired rapidly into the doorway where he would have been if he hadn't fallen left and down. The rounds were too close together to count, a roar of sound and smoke and it didn't matter. Nothing mattered but the two men.

He held the Smith with both hands and fired double-action, three at each man, as fast as he could pull the trigger and resettle the gun after recoil.

The first man went down as if swept by a wind, but the second one held, although Murphy could have sworn he hit him. The man swung his gun sideways and fired at Murphy again and Murphy felt the bullet take him across the top of the hip as he lay on his side. The impact rolled him back into the wall, and he dropped the Smith as it clicked empty and ripped the Colt's from his belt. He eared the hammer, held for a heartbeat, and aimed while the man fired at him again—he felt a sting this time from his ear and heard the bullet as it went by—and squeezed.

The bullet plowed across the top of the coarse wood bar and took the man in the middle of the stomach. He whooshed air and went back against the back bar, bottles falling around him. Murphy cocked and fired again, aiming carefully, hitting him in the center of his chest. Then he fired once more, again into his chest, though he was dead or dying.

Silence.

The smoke was so thick he could no longer see where the men had been. He stuck the Colt's back in his belt, retrieved the Smith and, still lying on his side, broke it and reloaded from his belt. Blood dripped down from his ear onto his neck—he felt the heat of it—and he looked at the hip wound but could see nothing but a tear in the fabric of his pants and the meat below the bone and blood welling out of the opening. It wasn't pumping.

"Who the hell are you?"

Murphy froze. The voice was high, seemed to come from above the smoke, and for the first time he realized there was a lower ceiling in the. back half, over him. There must be a loft and the man was up there. They had thought Murphy was coming in the front and they were going to get him from above as well as to the side.

He tried to locate the voice. Closed the Smith quietly, checked the cylinder. One of them rubbed and he broke it open and reset all the shells with his thumb, then closed it and checked it again.

"You from down in Kansas? We did that bit of work down there but I didn't think there was nobody left to follow us . . ."

Murphy thought he had it. Over to the right, and near the front of the loft. He held the Smith with both hands and fired all six in a rough oval, up through the floor and angled back to the right wall.

He heard a thud, then some scrambling and nothing more. He broke the Smith again, extracted the empties, which were jamming now in the powder residue, and reloaded from his belt. Each new shell had to be punched down with his thumb, and he knew if he fired another whole cylinder he would have trouble loading.

He'd have to move out, see the bastard so he could get a shot at him. Shooting up through the floor wouldn't get it done.

All this time he'd been lying on his side, and he rose to his feet carefully, trying to remain silent. His hip hurt now, as did the old wounds, and there was a sting in his ear. In front of him, out in the middle of the room but slightly to the left of center, there was a cast-iron potbellied stove. If he could make it to the stove and turn . . .

His thinking was stopped by sudden movement in front of the saloon. There were two sets of paned windows, one on each side of the open doorway, and he saw the old Indian move across one of the windows.

Almost as he saw the movement, fire erupted from overhead, and the right window shattered and the old man went down. Three shots came almost as one, and he saw a handgun come past the edge of the loft, smoke and fire blowing out as the man fired.

Murphy pulled the Smith up and fired three times through the loft floor, measuring back from the extended handgun, spacing the shots. On the third one the handgun above jerked and the hand holding it opened and the gun fell, and Murphy moved out into the open part of the floor and swung the Smith up, looking for a target.

He saw a man's face, looking over the edge of the loft. The leader of the riders. Darrin Teason. The man Murphy had hit in Casper. But even in the smoke he could see he had hit the man solidly. He was graying as his life went down.

"Casper—you're the one from Casper who hit me."

"The canyon," Murphy said. "The woman."

"What woman?"

Murphy was shaking with it. *The son of a bitch didn't even remember it.* "The horses," he said and shot the man in the face. "The woman with the horses."

There was a sudden roar from his rear and he turned to see the old man looking through the shattered window, aiming the rifle down in the back of the bar.

"One of them was still moving."

But Murphy didn't hear. He holstered the Smith and walked back out into the sun. He had work to do, riding to do before it was over.

"The horses," he said to the old man. "You can have them. Sell them to that buyer in the other saloon and use the money to keep you and your woman warm. I'll take the jenny and jack and some food."

He limped to the jenny across the street, mounted, and rode.

It was a ways back to Casper.

CHAPTER 19

HE reached Casper on the third day of riding, his hip on fire the first two and settling down the second. The bleeding stopped almost at once, and other than the pain—which was controllable if he rode slightly up on one cheek—it was a shallow wound.

There were things to do and then the ride back to the canyon. He needed a stone for Midge and he found a stonecutter at the edge of town. He had four blank stones and Murphy picked one small enough to pack on the mule the three days it would take to get to the canyon.

He gave the man Midge's name and approximate dates of birth and death—he knew neither one for certain—and asked for something about flowers because she liked flowers.

"That'll be ten dollars." The man said it as if he were saying ten thousand dollars, but Murphy had some coins in his right pocket and he paid the man with a twenty-dollar gold piece—his last one.

"Have it done in three hours," he told the cutter. "I'll be leaving then."

He then rode to the marshal's office and found the same kid. It surprised him to see the boy still there, and then he realized that not two weeks had passed since he was last here. He took some coffee when it was offered and settled into a chair.

"Those riders are done," he said, leaning back and

sipping coffee. His eyes idly scanned the wall, the gun rack.

"All of them?" The boy took some coffee as well. His face had hardened off but he still looked young. That would change. Soon. If he lived.

"All."

"Hiram was right—you're tougher than boiled owlshit."

The rifle. Murphy had been looking at it for two minutes and hadn't seen it. In the gun rack was a lever rifle with porcupine chewing on the handgrip. He stood and went to the gun rack and took the rifle down. The chew marks were exactly the same. It was his .45–70. Midge, he thought. Midge had her hand right here.

"Where did you get this?"

"The rifle? It came off an old prospector. He came into town just after you left and set to drinking and raising hell. Next thing anybody knew he took that rifle and started to shoot into the buildings up and down the street, and when I went out to stop him he turned it on me."

"Where is he now?"

"Dead. I shot him when he swung on me with it. Why? Do you know something about the gun?"

Murphy said nothing, looked out the window. Oh Christ, he thought—what if it wasn't the riders? Maybe it was one old man—and I killed and killed . . . one old man went up there and chased her and killed her and I didn't even know he was the one . . .

He touched the rifle where the porcupine had chewed it, remembering that day when they went to the stream-bed and fired. Just over two weeks ago. "It's my rifle. He must've stole it from my wo . . . my wife after he killed her."

"I'm sorry to hear that—that he killed your wife. I didn't know. I guess I'm glad I shot him then."

Murphy turned, carrying the rifle, and went out the door without speaking, his eyes burning. He had to grain the jenny and jack and get the stone and go back to the canyon.

There was that to do and nothing after that.

EPILOGUE

THE wagon was gone when he returned, and there had been a light rain so any tracks were wiped as well, but it didn't matter. He rode past where he'd left it, the jenny figuring she was going home now, the jack following eagerly, carrying the stone for Midge's grave on a pack-saddle Murphy had picked up in Casper.

He smelled the smoke before he cleared the cotton-woods entering the canyon. It was flat smoke, the flat smoke of cottonwood burning. Not the pungent odor of pine or brush. And in it something else, some other smell he couldn't quite place; and then he realized it was burned food. Corn. Burned cornbread and burned bacon.

Somebody was at the cabin, had a cook fire going. He pulled the .45–70 from the scabbard beneath his leg and held it across the saddle horn, jacked a round into the chamber, and let the hammer off.

When he cleared the cottonwoods along the stream and could see the cabin the first thing he saw were children. A boy and a girl were running in the shallow water at the edge of the pond, splashing each other.

Squatters. He slid the rifle back into the scabbard and rode up to the cabin.

The children stopped to watch him ride up. Not afraid so much as curious. Murphy saw his wagon next to the lean-to, also saw that everything had been cleaned up. There was a jersey cow in the corral. A cow, he thought—Midge had wanted to get a cow. And they had chickens. The garden was tended, weeded, clean and neat.

"Ma!" the boy yelled as he rode close. "Somebody's here on a mule!"

A woman came to the door of the cabin, red and burned in the face, red hands she was wiping on a piece of sacking. Why were they always red, he wondered. Almost as soon as she appeared a man came from around the back of the lean-to, holding a piece of harness trace he'd been mending.

There was a moment of silence as they all looked at one another.

"Welcome," the man said. "Would you like some cold water or hot coffee?"

"This is my place," Murphy said, and he knew as soon as the words were out that it wasn't true. It wasn't his place any longer. It had been Midge's place, his and Midge's place, but it was nothing now. A place to come and die.

"Oh—we didn't know. We found the wagon out there abandoned with some gear left in it and came up here and the place looked abandoned. If we'd have known you were coming back we wouldn't have moved in this way. But when Mary found the grave above the house she figured something bad had happened and the people had moved off."

"I put some flower seeds around the grave and watered them," the woman said. "It seemed so small and alone I thought the flowers might cheer it up. Was it your woman?"

Murphy didn't answer. He got off the jenny and dropped the reins and the boy came forward to hold her, though there was no need. The jenny would stand now for hours, would steer to his knees, listen for his voice. She was like a sister. A little sister. He led the jack with the stone back around the cabin and up to the grave. It only took him a moment to mount the stone base and put the stone on it. The carver had put a spray of granite flowers on the face of the stone, with Midge's name, and IN BEAUTY SHE SLEEPS across the middle of the stone in capital letters.

He did not feel sadness. He had a moment of piercing, intense loss—a knife pushed through him—and it was gone. He saw that the woman's flowers were up in little seedlings and he touched one of them, small and frail.

He stood.

"You stay," he said to the family as he went past the cabin. They had not followed him up to the grave. "It's your place. Tend the grave and put flowers in each spring and it's your place and your wagon. Oh, there might come an old Indian man and his woman to winter here. If you could I'd appreciate you helping him build a cabin and letting him stay and be warm. I owe him."

He said no more, nor did they; but they watched as he mounted the jenny and rode away, down through the aspens and cottonwoods and out of sight. The neglected jack stood watching them leave, and when he couldn't see them any longer he brayed, pawed twice, and couldn't stand it.

He took off at a lope, the packsaddle flapping, holding his head out to the side to keep from stepping on the rope.

If you have enjoyed this book and would like to receive details of other Walker Western titles, please write to:

Western Editor
Walker and Company
720 Fifth Avenue
New York, NY 10019

W   L

AUG 1 1 1989

Regular loan : 2 weeks
A daily fine is charged for each overdue book.
Books may be renewed once, unless reserved
for another patron.
A borrower is responsible for books damaged
or lost while charged on his card